Pine needles were scattered across the top of the car. From the incident, the road rash had resulted in a half-bare tree.

Standing, Dominic wiped his hands on the back of his jeans. His six-pack abs flexed and Waverly averted her eyes toward the tree. The timber was safe from getting run over, thanks to the abandoned road Dominic had thought to take. His eyes followed hers. "I'm getting you another tree. We're tossing this."

Before he took another step toward the road, Waverly reached for Dominic's arm. His bicep twitched beneath her palm. "I don't need a tree."

Dominic paused for a moment. Their eyes locked. Suddenly the tree was no longer in question. Waverly's heart raced. Her feelings, jumbled with the longing for what the Harveys had and wanting it with Dominic, came into mind.

"What is it you need, Waverly?"

"I— I—" The words were lost but the action was not. Waverly leaped forward and threw herself into Dominic's arms. He caught her and spun her body around, placing her back against the hood.

Dear Reader,

Waverly Leverve has always had a passion for beauty pageants and bad boys. At one point in her life, her mother feared the latter would ruin her chances for the ultimate tiara. Eventually, Waverly's mouth got her in trouble. Can you imagine having your ugly-cry face captured and placed on a viral meme for the world to see and use for their entertainment? Welcome to Waverly's new world. What's a dethroned pageant gal to do? Step back into the tiara of course.

I had a blast imagining all the memes of Waverly's ugly cry. A lot of my inspiration came from a particular "crying meme" of a legendary basketball player.

Until the next pageant…happy reading!

Carolyn Hector

A Tiara Under the Tree

Carolyn Hector

HARLEQUIN® KIMANI™ ROMANCE

Recycling programs
for this product may
not exist in your area.

ISBN-13: 978-0-373-86524-6

A Tiara Under the Tree

HARLEQUIN®

www.Harlequin.com

Printed in U.S.A.

Having your story read out loud as a teen by your brother in Julia Child's voice might scare some folks from ever sharing their work. But **Carolyn Hector** rose above her fear. She currently resides in Tallahassee, Florida, where there is never a dull moment. School functions, politics, football, Southern charm and sizzling heat help fuel her knack for putting a romantic spin on everything she comes across. Find out what she's up to on Twitter: @Carolyn32303.

Books by Carolyn Hector

Harlequin Kimani Romance

The Magic of Mistletoe
The Bachelor and the Beauty Queen
His Southern Sweetheart
The Beauty and the CEO
A Tiara Under the Tree

Visit the Author Profile page
at Harlequin.com for more titles.

I would like to dedicate and acknowledge my editor, Carly Silver, and her magical editing squad. I say this with my most sincere pageant wave and ugly cry— THANK YOU.

Acknowledgments

I would like to acknowledge my Destin Divas for their entertainment, friendship and wisdom.

Chapter 1

Death by chocolate. Waverly Leverve licked the dark, shiny ganache off her fingertip until she cleaned her finger down to her chipped French manicure. Biting her bottom lip, Waverly glanced over the double cupcakes standing proudly on the crisp white china plate and settled on a Slow Torture Southern Peach Cobbler Cupcake.

For the last week Waverly had tried to wallow in self-pity and fatty foods. Why not? Any career as the future Miss Georgia and eventually Miss USA disappeared the moment officials forced her to give up her Miss South Georgia crown. So what if she'd colorfully told off a reporter? The journalist deserved her outburst. He'd propositioned her, assuming she was a naive pageant girl and when Waverly reacted, no one wanted to hear her side. He was the one with the recording. In hindsight, Waverly's idea wasn't a bright one, to tell a mic-ed reporter that the pageant establishment did not offer her enough money to sit around and smile in his face. There were a few *f* words dropped, along with her telling the man to self-fornicate. She should have just explained she was tired. Now here she sat in a bakery, shoveling carbs into her body.

The pink bejeweled cell phone rattled against the silver two-top table in the corner of The Cupcakery. Waverly flipped the gadget over and blinked back at the turquoise-blue screen and fat black letters.

You can't drown yourself in food.

"Want to bet?" Waverly asked the phone. Her snarky response garnered the attention of the pretty cashier at the counter.

"Did you say something?" Tiffani asked her question from behind the register. The late-afternoon sun glinted off the arched glass protecting the cupcake display and shining against Tiffani's face in a golden glow.

Waverly shook her head. Tendrils falling from her messy bun tickled the back of her neck. "I'm just talking to my cell."

"Is that one of those phones you can see the person you're talking to on?"

It was, but these days Waverly turned the feature off. The only person calling her was her mother. Jillian Leverve hated the idea of her daughter having to give up her tiara for the antics provoked by an angry journalist, but in the end she hated even more the derailed plans for the highest crown the two of them had dreamed of ever since Waverly walked in her first toddler pageant.

"Not this time, Tiffani," Waverly said.

"You think after you finish we can work on my pageant wave and walk?"

Another ding sounded and Waverly's phone lit up. Waverly expected a motivational quote from her tiara squad, her group of friends who understood the pageant life. Waverly picked a peach from her cupcake and savored the fruit while she read her text.

Remember, someone once said good girls seldom make history... Come and be a contestant in the pageant. The ladies are just gathering tonight. You won't miss a thing.

Waverly responded with two letters. N-o.

At least come to the pageant and help if you insist on not participating...

And be around other people achieving what she'd failed? *No, thanks.* She scoffed to herself. Waverly turned her frown into a smile and grinned at the cashier. The last person she wanted to piss off was the only person not judging her for the dethroning ceremony: the cashier who supplied her with cupcakes. "Sounds like a plan to me," said Waverly to herself.

Wallowing in her self-pity, Waverly cleared the text with her frosting-covered finger and took another glance at the latest meme. This one today captured Waverly's ugly-cry face as she tearfully handed over her sparkly Miss South Georgia crown. The meme in question superimposed her body onto a basketball court. While her hands were on her crown, the star basketball player on the court blocked her crown as if it was a basketball.

Part of the deal for becoming Miss Georgia meant a contestant needed to maintain residency in the state for six months. Six weeks into laying her foundation and all hell broke loose. Instead of going home to her mother's in Florida, Waverly sought refuge in the town of Southwood, Georgia, a small town just above the Florida border. Well, hell, since her dreams were placed on hold, why not give a few pointers for this weekend's big pageant?

"Are you sure you don't want to try out?" asked Tiffani. "Don't you need the Miss Southwood title more than me?"

If only... Waverly thought with a frown. Talk about a conflict of interest. The sender of the recent texts was not just Lexi Pendergrass Reyes, but *the* Lexi Pendergrass Reyes, hostess of the Miss Southwood Beauty Pageant. The former beauty queen had herself survived vicious pageant rumors back in her reign surrounding a particularly revealing low-cut dress she designed combined with an inappropriate relationship with a pageant dad, and ended up with the last laugh.

In order to win a pageant, a contestant needed one of two things: a dress from Lexi's store, Grits and Glam Gowns, or Lexi as a pageant coach. Lexi had coached Waverly when she first started out in pageants, and Waverly wore several of Lexi's gowns. Any girl wearing a Lexi design won her title. But there would be too many things wrong with Waverly entering Lexi's pageant. They were close personal friends, she didn't have a dress and having been dropped by the pageant committee for Miss South Georgia, she had no sponsor—hence her factors hindering her road to the bigger title.

Depressed even more, Waverly picked up her fork and began digging into the Slow Torture Southern dessert. Chunks of vibrant, orange-tinted peaches clung to the sweet interior of the cupcake. The sweetness of the buttery frosting melted against her tongue.

"Hey, you know what?" Tiffani exclaimed with a curtsy. "When you're done with the peach cupcake, I have one left for you."

"You do?" Waverly finished the rest of her cupcake and scooted back in her seat. Licking the frosting off her finger, she headed toward the counter. Another chocolate cupcake would be dinner. In the time it took Waverly to stand up and get her plate together, Tiffani disappeared behind the black-and-white polka-dot French doors leading into the kitchen. Waverly sauntered to the counter and lingered over the curved glass. The varieties of the cupcakes tempted her. Her mouth watered at the rows. The dark chocolate with peanut butter frosting, the vanilla drizzled with caramel, the salted caramel, the chocolate wafer cookie and even the birthday cake cupcake with pastel sprinkles all tempted her.

Distracted by the hungry howl of her stomach, Waverly didn't realize the bells over the bakery's door had jingled until she saw the shadow of a figure blocking the blinding sun off the glass. He motioned for her to go ahead of him. Waverly turned to offer her thanks and to step out of the way for the customer since her order was on its way. Waverly's mouth watered…and not from the yummy smells coming from the kitchen.

Over six feet tall with broad shoulders and bulky muscles poured into a dark gray suit with a yellow-and-gray paisley tie stood in front of her. The man oozed sex appeal and confirmed his status with a sexy, lop-sided grin.

"Hello," the deep, velvet voice crooned.

"Hi," Waverly said, or at least she believed she did. It was hard to hear over the pounding of her heart against her rib cage. In the past, Waverly's taste in men leaned more toward the obvious bad boys—the biker-guy type riddled with tattoos, ripped jeans, snug T-shirts and a reputation a mile long. One bad-boy boyfriend in particular had once got her banned from a pageant. Now, with nothing but time on her hands, Waverly might need to give men in suits a chance, just like carbs. And carbohydrates were delicious.

The man extended his copper-colored hand toward the counter. "By all means. You were here first."

"Oh, no." Waverly stumbled over her words. "I already know what I want."

The man wiggled his brows. "A woman who knows what she wants? Nice."

"Don't be surprised," said Waverly. "It's not so hard to choose."

"Not for me," he responded. "I am here for one thing only."

A jolt of electricity raced through Waverly. She pressed her lips together and, for the first time in a week, feared her looks. This wallowing-in-misery thing had allowed her to walk around in sweats, makeup-free, hair unkempt.

"The Slow Torture Southern Peach Cobbler Cupcake," he announced.

Two odd feelings washed over Waverly. Jealousy and greed. Odd to envy a cupcake, right? For some reason she wished this stranger had meant wanting her. And now to realize they both stood at the counter wanting the same cupcake...

The French doors opened and Tiffani appeared with a bright red shade of lipstick Waverly had failed to notice earlier. If she wasn't mistaken, Tiffani wore one of Waverly's favorites—Go Get Him Red by Ravens Cosmetics. Waverly cocked her head to the side as she noticed the way Tiffani tried to control her rapid breathing. She recognized this tactic and had perfected it often when the backstage lineup changed at pageants. The cashier batted her lashes at the man.

"You're back."

Waverly took a step to the side. Clearly this was a tender moment between two long-lost acquaintances, right? How dare he flirt with Waverly at his lady friend's place of business? Waverly frowned.

"You know The Cupcakery was my first stop."

"And I have exactly what you want." Tiffani awkwardly reached to the left while maintaining eye contact with the new customer.

"Ah, my Peach Cobbler cupcake."

"Hey, wait a minute," Waverly said, stepping forward. "That's mine."

"You already had one." Tiffani turned to Waverly with a cold smile.

Hand pressed to her heart, Waverly gasped. "But..."

"You've already eaten one," Tiffani repeated, "and you still have another one on your plate. Don't be greedy. This gentleman has traveled far just for this." She held the plate in the air. Waverly watched as a crumb fell to the ground, much like her heart right now.

"If you already ordered this," said the man, "by all means, have it."

"No," Waverly said, shaking her head. "I probably need to watch my figure."

The man leaned toward the right for a better look at Waverly's backside. She'd been in beauty pageants in nothing but a bikini and heels, yet she'd never felt more like a piece of meat than right now. Waverly bit her bottom lip, not sure if she needed to be offended. Given the way she'd been eating her feelings and comforting herself over poor choices, Waverly felt heavy. With the recent weight gain, his lone raised brow of approval thrilled her.

Tiffani cleared her throat. The man shook his head and gave his attention to the cashier. Waverly took the moment to walk back to her table. To prevent further embarrassment, Waverly kept walking, straight into the ladies' bathroom. In private, away from prying eyes, the man's in particular, Waverly clung to the clean white counter. The coolness of the marble chilled her palms, soothing the heat that rose inside her soul and tinted her cheeks a deep pink. In her quest for the tiara, Waverly had let dating fall by the wayside. Her last serious boyfriend was four years ago. Johnny Del Vecchio. He was her first crush, first everything. The local bad boy had swept Waverly off her feet and onto his motorcycle. His street racing antics helped call attention to the pageant committees and shine a spotlight on her tightrope walk on the bad side. The desire for the tiara eventually lured Waverly onto the right path.

Once her sun-kissed tan began to return, Waverly took a deep breath and headed back out into the dining area. In any other city, she would have taken her belongings with her, but Waverly knew her cupcake and classified ads were okay. The only thing different at her table was the black-and-white polka-dot box next to her plate. She immediately recognized the to-go carton, since she'd brought several home with her over the last two weeks. Waverly glanced toward Tiffani in question, only to be given a dramatic eye roll. Safe to say Tiffani wouldn't be needing personal guidance with the pageant this evening. Waverly fingered the bow at the top of the box to loosen the card.

"It's yours."

She couldn't. Waverly scooped up her belongings and headed out the door. Sunlight blinded her momentarily until she shielded her eyes with her hand. She wasn't in the bathroom so long that she'd missed the stranger. Waverly didn't see him in the first direction she looked, but found him the other way, at the corner.

"Hey," Waverly called out to him. "Sir?"

The man turned toward Waverly. He wore a pair of silver aviator glasses. "Did you get my card? My name is on the back."

Flipping the card over, Waverly silently read the raised letters. Dominic Crowne, Crowne's Garage. "Well, Mr. Crowne, I can't take this," Waverly said, shoving the box out to him. He held his large hands toward her and shook his head. "At least we can share. Maybe we can go inside and get a knife."

"First of all, the name is Dominic, and second," he said with a wink, "I don't share. *Anything.*"

His deep voice and blatant flirt sent a chill down her spine in the summer heat. "You're pretty bold, *Dominic.*"

"Because I offered you the last cupcake?" Dominic asked. "Most people say I'm chivalrous."

"You're flirting with me when your girlfriend is in there." Waverly nodded toward the bakery.

"Who, Tiffani?" Dominic's deep voice rose an octave. "Why would you…? Never mind. There's been a misunderstanding."

"Obviously," said Waverly, still pushing the cupcake toward his massive, broad chest.

"Tiffani is a family friend."

Did Tiffani realize they were just friends? Still new to Southwood, Waverly didn't know what families were related or who everyone's best friend was. Waverly knew a handful of people—Lexi and her family and then, of course, Jolene, Lexi's cousin and Waverly's former roommate at Cypress Boarding School for Girls. What she did know was Tiffani's kindness to her. Clearly the girl had a crush…understandably.

"Friends." Waverly mimicked his word.

"Yes," Dominic confirmed. He pressed the cupcake back toward Waverly. Their hands brushed and a spark was set off between them. Waverly took a step backward. He took a step toward her. "Do us both a favor—give me a call."

Waverly stood still, her heart beating rapidly against her rib cage until Dominic Crowne crossed the street and disappeared into the crowd of pedestrians. She pondered whether to toss the business card and the cupcake into the trash. The last thing she needed right now was a relationship. No, she said to herself, the best thing for her was to focus on a new set of goals and get back on track to achieving her ultimate dream, Miss USA, starting with obtaining the Miss Georgia title. After Waverly's heartbeat returned to a normal state, she made a drastic decision…she decided to keep the cupcake.

"You're back sooner than I expected." Alisha Crowne glanced up from her stack of magazines—not quite the welcome reception he expected from his little sister.

Dominic turned the open sign over to close the garage, disappointed there wasn't a line of cars in the driveway, but there were two in the lift and that meant something. At least they weren't the same ones up there when Dominic had left for Dubai two weeks ago.

"Will Ravens flew into town for some event," Dominic explained and ignored the dreamy sigh Alisha made at the sound of his fraternity brother's name. Dominic's frat brother Will recently became the CEO of his family's corporation, Ravens Cosmetics, and was in town for some event. "Where is everyone?" Dominic asked, looking around.

He'd opened Crowne's Garage in Southwood in hopes of getting the townsfolk to come here rather than his ranch. Growing up poor in Miami, Florida, Dominic had known his mother could not afford to bring their hunk of junk to a mechanic every month, nor could she afford a newer car. At a young age Dominic learned how to fix the family vehicle. Eventually Dominic opened up his own garage. Miami was too busy and crowded for his classic car collection and the ranch land in Southwood seemed like a perfect place to relocate. A write-up in the local paper sent people in town to his place and flooded his driveway with cars needing routine services. In order to keep his privacy, Dominic opened up a shop in town. He liked restoring vehicles.

Twenty-one-year-old Alisha blew a bubble with her bright pink gum and shrugged. "I mean, I told everyone to leave."

"Why?"

"Because there's nothing to do here and there's a whole kickball-slip-n-slide tournament going on right now."

Dominic bit the inside of his cheek to keep from saying anything too rash. He'd made the decision when he moved to Southwood six months ago to bring his party-going sister with him. Their mother, Angela, was at her wit's end with Alisha. She wasn't in school and hung out with a fast crowd in Miami. Ten years older than his sister, Dominic had become the surrogate father to Alisha and their brothers, Dario and Darren, when their father left them. Dario and Darren were at least on the right path in life and in college, even if it were every other semester, and staying out of trouble…usually.

"And what about the cars here?" Dominic hiked his thumb toward the vehicles in the air.

"Gee, Dom, the parts haven't arrived in the mail like we expected," Alisha said through a forced smile. She picked up a stack of letters. "I know what I'm doing."

Because the stack in her hands was so thick, Dominic questioned her last statement. "I ordered the parts three weeks ago, before I left."

"I know." Alisha handed Dominic the stack of mail addressed to him. "And I need you to go through these as soon as possible. You never responded to the District Planning Committee about sponsoring a contestant."

Dominic's left eye twitched as he wondered what his sister was talking about. "What?"

"There is a beauty pageant this coming weekend and I know you want to put up a few more garages in town."

"Okay?" Dominic said, humming to himself. No one could compare to the beauty he'd met this afternoon—sort of met. He never caught her name, but Dominic promised himself once he did, he'd never forget it. The cupcake girl was unlike any woman Dominic had met in a while. After spending two weeks in Dubai and enticed with vapid, gorgeous women who ate nothing but lettuce, Dominic enjoyed seeing a woman with a healthy appetite. Having practically raised Alisha, Dominic was well aware of how women behaved around men. Alisha and her friends pigged out at home but pretended to be on diets on dates.

The trip to Dubai had been half pleasure and half business. His other college friend Aamir Assadi requisitioned Dominic's help with a few vehicles and insisted he come to Dubai to deliver them personally. Aamir sent his private plane for Dominic and set him up in his family's high-rise condominium. When he learned Will planned on coming to Southwood, Dominic wasn't heartbroken to cut his time overseas short to accommodate Will's arrival. Owning three different garages and two restoration shops in South Florida allowed Dominic to expand up north, to serve a larger clientele without distraction from city life. Dominic had purchased a ranch-style home on the outskirts of Southwood. The large space of open pavement was a huge selling point for test-driving the horsepower of his restored vehicles. In emergency cases, he might be asked to use the paved land for life-flight helicopters. Dominic kept the strip clear of parked cars, so landing on the makeshift airstrip had cut down on travel time for Will and hopefully opened up time for the friends to hang out and catch up.

"Tiffani still needs a sponsor."

Dominic did not need his sister's fast best friend thinking there was a future for them. Sponsoring her would not clarify things. "Tiffani's parents own The Cupcakery. Why aren't they sponsoring her?"

"They are, but if you're willing—"

"I'm not." Dominic cut her off. "I don't have time for a pageant or the drama of one, Alisha. Try again." He pushed away from the counter and headed off toward his office.

"You need to become more involved with the community," Alisha hollered after him. "Folks are still bringing their cars to the mechanic in Peachville. Tiffani knows people. She can be an asset."

Dominic let the glass door close without a care about the rattling frame. A sigh of relief escaped from the back of his throat. No more hotel rooms. No more surprise visitors knocking on the door. While Dominic wasn't the best cook, he at least would have something he made without feeling guilty for all the richness… maybe even a protein shake, and then he'd hit the gym. Dominic strolled over to his desk, wondering why he didn't stay home. When Aamir's private plane landed on Dominic's property to drop him off, he should have just stayed home instead of coming in to check on the garage. Alas, Dominic knew he came because the garage was his baby.

The walls in Dominic's office were adorned with pictures of some of his work: the first car he'd restored, the celebrities he worked with and the first garage he opened up when he turned twenty. Not bad for a kid who almost dropped out of high school. Dominic glanced up at his diploma, framed by his family. His mother had been so proud to have a son earn a full scholarship to Stanford, especially when they grew up on the wrong side of the tracks.

A stack of paperwork teetered on the corner of his custom-designed desk. The hood of the 1969 Camaro had been stripped from the rest of the body and turned into a desk in a twisted form of revenge from an old friend of his who'd found his car-loving wife with another man. Dominic stretched before sitting down. The door to his locker room was still closed, but he knew his coveralls were waiting for him. He'd spent the last two weeks showing off the Ferrari and Porsches he customized for Aamir, but now he was ready to get started working beneath the hood of any of the cars. Being underneath a four-thousand-pound car soothed him.

Instead of getting up to change, Dominic sat and decompressed. His mind went back to the woman at The Cupcakery. For once Dominic wished he'd listened to Alisha and got more involved with the community. He sponsored Little League games. Several peewee baseball teams bore the Crowne's Garage logo on the backs of their shirts. He never went to a game long enough to get to know anyone, though. Growing up and taking care of everyone in his family had never left time for Dominic to socialize. Alisha, on the other hand, had been out the first weekend she moved here. In order to keep her safe and from driving out to his ranch so late at night, Dominic bought Alisha a condo within walking distance of the garage. The two-bedroom place worked out fine for him as well when he worked later than expected in the garage.

Rapid, hard knocks banged against the glass and the door opened before Dominic had a chance to say anything. Alisha appeared in the doorway, hand on her hip.

"Please," Dominic said, waving her inside. She didn't budge but instead huffed. "What?"

"I'm heading out now."

"Okay?" Dominic asked in a slow drawl.

"You forgot, didn't you?"

Dominic returned Alisha's huff. "Apparently so. What's up?"

"You were going to watch your nephew this evening."

By *nephew*, Alisha meant her teacup pig, Hamilton. Dominic wiped his hands down his face. "Alisha, I just returned."

"Yes, from a vacation without me while I stayed here and ran the garage," she reminded him. "When you told me how long you were going without me, you promised me the minute you got back you'd babysit. And you're back. Perfect timing, too."

"Alisha."

"Dominic," Alisha whined and bobbed her knee—the telltale sign of an adult temper tantrum. "C'mon. I won't be out long. I'll even buy you a pizza."

With his stomach rumbling, Dominic was sold. But he couldn't let Alisha know. "Fine, I'll do it."

"Good," his sister squealed. "I'm going to leave to get ready. I'll see you in a few?"

"I suppose."

There were a few things Dominic needed to go through before leaving. He preferred to go straight home, but a promise was a promise. His father, John, made the biggest promise ever and let everyone down.

"I'll be back" was more than a line from a futuristic cyborg. The last words John had said to the family had stuck with Dominic forever. He hated to let anyone down, especially anyone he cared for. Dominic flipped through his mail and spotted the familiar return address from an Arizona home. Like he did with the other letters he received since setting up shop in Southwood, he threw it away.

Dominic lingered in the office for a little bit while Alisha and her friend got ready at her condo. He saw no need to sit in Alisha's frilly living room and dodge Tiffani's attempts at flirting. It wasn't like Tiffani wasn't pretty—she was—but she was also his sister's good friend, which meant she had a lot of qualities like Alisha. Dominic wanted a woman with goals in life. Alisha cared about the next party and Dominic blamed himself for always indulging in her demands. His mind wandered to the woman at the bakery as he lifted his hand to knock on his sister's door. He shook his head at the idea of asking the cupcake woman if she wanted to get paid to stand around and look pretty at some pageant.

The door opened before Dominic had a chance to knock. A wave of scent from a sweet-smelling candle swooshed through the opening of the door. Tiffani popped her head out.

"I thought I heard the elevator."

Alisha lived in one of the newer condominiums in Southwood. It was built in a square with a courtyard down below in the center. The elevator closer to Alisha's place was out of commission. The other elevator was down the hall on the other side. How Tiffani had heard the elevator when he took the steps was beyond him. Had she seen him pull into the parking lot from Alisha's balcony?

Rather than embarrass her, he nodded. "Yep, that was me."

A pink teacup pig wearing a pink tutu wedged his snout in the door crack. Tiffani stepped aside to let Dominic in. Once Hamilton finished sniffing him, he began to hop around Dominic's black boots. A load of laundry tumbled in the dryer in the room to the right of the foyer. Dominic proceeded down the hall, passing the guest bedroom he slept in on the nights he worked too late and the kitchen to the left. The island bar was home to a number of expensive bottles of wine. A pile of folded laundry sat on the edge of Alisha's glass-top table. In the living room Dominic found clothes on top of the long pink-and-gray-plaid couch. The gray recliner was covered with a pink blanket with Hamilton's toys. The only thing open was a love seat. With Tiffani hot on his tail, Dominic chose to stand in the center of the living room and play it off as if he wanted to check out the view from the glass doors leading out onto the balcony.

"So, how's business?"

Small talk. Great. "Business is fine," Dominic answered politely. "I'm guessing since there was one peach cupcake left, business is good for you, too?"

"Oh, yes, my mama is pleased with the sales."

Dominic nodded in agreement. In his research of where to set up shop, Southwood's business scene was exploding with mom-and-pop shops. The only thing not growing was the club scene, and Dominic was fine with that. The sooner the ladies left, the sooner they'd return and Dominic could get back to the ranch.

"I should have made a new batch for you tonight," Tiffani suggested.

"No, really." Dominic shook his head and patted his gut. "I don't need any more."

"Any more? You gave the last one away," Tiffani shrieked. The corners of her mouth turned down in a frown.

With perfect timing, Alisha strolled into the living room. The outfit she wore, half a black dress that stopped just at her butt and black stiletto heels, was best suited for a nightclub in Miami and, considering she was his little sister, best on someone else. "Gave away a cupcake? Are you nuts?"

"Some new girl in town," supplied Tiffani with an eye roll.

Alisha looked up at Dominic. "You met a girl?" Alisha's voice dripped with pride.

"I'm not Quasimodo, Alisha."

"No, you're not," said Tiffani.

"I didn't say you were," Alisha said, playfully punching him in the arm. "Why didn't you tell me you met a girl? When do I get to meet her? What does she do around here?"

Dominic grabbed Alisha's fist and tapped her on the shoulder. "This is exactly why I don't tell you things. You guys go on and enjoy your evening."

Alisha pouted for a moment before grabbing her clutch out from under the pile of clothes on the couch. "I ordered a pizza. My favorite, so I expect there to be leftovers."

"You eat a whole pie once or twice and suddenly people start claiming their own." Dominic chuckled.

"I'm serious," warned Alisha. "And Hamilton has an order of carrots and celery coming, too."

The pig got to eat healthier than the people. Hamilton squeaked at Dominic's feet. Dominic bent down and heavy-handedly petted the thing. "Why do you have a tutu on him?"

"Because a tuxedo would look silly." Alisha sighed and nudged Tiffani forward so they could leave.

Alone in the living room, Dominic glanced around for the remote control. By the time he found it underneath the third cushion, the doorbell rang. He figured it had to be the pizza—Alisha's favorite pizza, spinach Alfredo. He'd half expected Alisha to leave him with the bill, but the delivery guy said the pizza was paid for and left without waiting on a cash tip. She probably felt guilty for asking him to babysit Hamilton. Of course, Dominic thought with a chuckle, if she really wanted to make things right, she would have ordered a double-pepperoni pizza.

Dominic set the extra-large box on the counter. From the smell alone he knew the order was wrong. This was a double pepperoni, not what Alisha ordered. He raised his brow in question, wondering if Alisha had pulled a fast one on him and really got him his favorite. Who was he kidding? She mentioned she wanted her leftovers. And Hamilton's dinner was missing, as well. Dominic tilted the box up to see the name on the order. Lexi Pendergrass Reyes, apartment 501.

If he wasn't mistaken, Lexi was married and living in the suburbs. Last fall he'd serviced a beautiful 1952 Fiat 8V. The car had been a present from Lexi to her husband, Stephen Reyes, who happened to be the same man who sold him the ranch. They were nice people, but Dominic knew they didn't live here. With a huff, Dominic grabbed the cardboard box and turned to Hamilton. "I'll be right back with our food."

Hamilton squealed an answer and then, with a snort, turned back toward the living room, spun around three times and collapsed on a pile of clothes on the floor. Dominic shook his head and walked out the door. He found apartment 501 on the other side of the building. Had he realized, he could have gone into the bedroom and called out from the courtyard-side balcony.

Loud music thumped down the hallway. The Reyes family had two girls. Was one of them old enough to be throwing a party? Dominic found himself in a dilemma. Did he stop the party from going on or did he at least make the pizza exchange? He preferred going against a teenager than dealing with Alisha's wrath when she came home in a few hours to the wrong pizza.

Three brass numbers stood between Dominic and the pizza. Savoring the moments with the best pizza in the world, Dominic reluctantly knocked on the door. The music shut off. The sound of bare feet padding across the hardwood floor neared the door. He expected several people. With a whoosh the door swung open. Almond-shaped eyes widened at the sight of him. Long, lean and slender spilled out from a pair of black stretchy shorts, which hugged her curvy hips. Instead of the bun she wore earlier, a twelve-inch diamond crown was on top of her dark hair.

"Cupcake Girl?"

Chapter 2

"Dominic Crowne?" Waverly breathed the man's name and hoped to slow down the quickening pulse zipping through her veins. Since she'd seen him last, he'd shed the tailored suit and replaced it with jeans—a pair of well-fitted jeans—and a T-shirt. Tattoos covered his arms. She tried not to stare too hard. He might as well have come with a neon sign that read DANGER. Excitement coursed through her veins.

Dominic leaned against the door frame with a pizza box propped within the crook of his arm and against his hip. A dangerous smile, accompanied with a quick wiggle of his brow, crossed his face. "You're not Lexi."

"This is her place," Waverly explained. "Lexi is letting me crash here for a while."

"Crash here for a while?" He frowned. "Is your place being painted or something?"

Waverly shook her head and rolled her eyes. "Are you volunteering or something?"

"Maybe the 'something' part." Dominic licked his lips, and Waverly forgot about the howling in her stomach from a few minutes ago before pizza arrived. She stepped backward into the foyer of her apartment and caught a glimpse of her pink-tinted cheeks in the large gold-framed mirror by the door.

Waverly cleared her throat. "So, do you normally walk the halls with pizzas?"

"Oh, my bad." He shoved the pizza toward her. "You haven't looked at yours yet, have you?"

"I was about to sit down."

"Right after the crowning?" Dominic asked and pointed toward the top of her head.

Heat filled her cheeks. She cocked her head to the side, untangled the combs holding her tiara in place and released her unruly hair. "Sorry, I was just…"

Dominic held up his free hand. "It's okay. You had that second cupcake today—it was worth celebrating, I understand."

Waverly decided not to expose her greed and tell him she'd eaten a total of three cupcakes today. "Thanks." She laughed lightly. "You said something about a pizza?"

As if remembering the food in his arms, Dominic blinked and inhaled deeply while he nodded. "The delivery guy mixed up the apartment numbers. My sister lives across the courtyard and she's going to kill me if I don't leave her any leftovers. She only bought the one, even though I'm here to do a favor for her."

With widened eyes, Waverly bobbed her head from side to side. She took a step forward into the hallway and peered into the steaming-hot box for a peek of a double-pepperoni pie. "I wonder what I got. What other pizza could there be?"

"Jesus, now more than ever I need to know your name," Dominic groaned, pressing his hand against his chest. "At least I need to know your first name. Your last name isn't necessary."

She cocked her hand on her hip and laughed. "Why is my last name not necessary?"

"Because it's about to change to mine."

"At least let me hyphenate it," Waverly responded with a laugh. "Waverly Leverve-Crowne."

"As long as we can eat double pepperoni and cupcakes every day."

How was she supposed to just take her pizza from him without offering some of hers? Waverly opened her door wider and waved him inside. Taking the cue, Dominic strolled in. His walk was cocky, and he was confidently aware of his sexual prowess. Waverly inhaled deeply and shook her head. Something about this seemed wrong…but when was she ever known to make the right decisions?

"The pizza is in the kitchen," said Waverly. She walked passed him, bumping her shoulder against his hard biceps. Steam still rose from the cracks of the large square box. Stepping away from the kitchen gave herself the chance to realize she hadn't been able to smell the spicy pepperoni. Now she caught a whiff of the Alfredo. Chicken Alfredo was good—on a plate of pasta. On a pizza? Waverly frowned. "Does your sister like you?"

Dominic came around the island bar of her kitchen. He set her box on the counter next to the fraudulent pizza. "Depends on her mood. I'm guessing she doesn't tonight."

"What a shame you don't share things, because I feel so horrible for you not having a normal pizza." Glad to be in the presence of someone who appreciated a classic pizza, Waverly grinned. She attempted to pull the box closer to her side of the counter, but Dominic held on to one corner with a finger and stopped her.

"Well, hold on now." His left brow rose and matched the amused smile spreading across his handsome face. "Didn't I say there were exceptions?"

"No, but I'm guessing one of them is for pizza?"

"For you," he said with a wink, "I'll make the exception."

The line was corny, yet Waverly laughed—not just laughed but giggled. "I feel so honored."

"Well, it'd be my honor to dine with the queen," said Dominic, grabbing the tiara from her hand. A shocking overprotective sensation washed over her. This might have been what new mothers felt when someone held their newborn babies. The sparkly band looked so tiny and fragile in Dominic's large, rough hands.

Waverly touched the crown with her fingers. Having it on top of her head was natural. With it off her head, she felt anxious. Tonight she'd planned on having a date night with herself. "Sorry," Waverly mumbled and took the crown from his hand. She placed it back on top of her head where it belonged.

"Do you always wear a crown?" Dominic asked. He squinted his light brown eyes at her. "Was I so blinded by your beauty earlier that I didn't notice?"

"No," Waverly replied and moved toward the cabinets. She reached for the blue-and-white-patterned plates from the cupboard above the sink. She got up on tiptoe. Warmth oozed down her body when Dominic appeared behind her to help guide a plate down. Dominic took it from her hands and set it on the counter next to the one she had already taken out for herself. "I wasn't expecting company this evening, and I'd already reserved a table for a pity party of one."

"Now, what would a woman like you be doing with a table like that?" Dominic leaned against the counter as if he belonged there. And he did, as odd as it sounded. The blue Victorian accents on the cookie, flour and sugar jars in the kitchen made Dominic look like a bull in a china shop.

"If I told you, you'd think I'm crazy." Waverly chuckled. She motioned for Dominic to have a seat at the counter with her. Dominic opened the large lid to the pizza. Pepperoni-scented steam rose through the air. "Would you care for a beer?"

For a moment Dominic pressed his hands to his bowed head. She wondered if he was religious and praying before his meal. "Dear Lord, thank you for bringing this woman before me. Smart, beautiful, seemingly sane if you don't count the tiara and drinks beer? Not sure what I've done to deserve this, but thank you."

Waverly shook her head. The left side of her face tightened with her half smile. "You're crazy." Quickly she grabbed two bottled beers from the door of the fridge and kicked it closed before returning to her guest. She set the bottles down as Dominic began to serve the pizza.

"Then we're the perfect pair," said Dominic. "One slice or two?"

"Are you going to judge me if I put two slices together for a pizza sandwich?" Waverly asked, adjusting her invention. In midserve, Dominic dropped a slice onto the floor, dug his keys from his front pocket and pretended to push himself away from the counter. Was he shocked? Turned off? "Too disgusting?"

"No, not at all." He laughed. "I'm bringing you in front of the justice of the peace right now."

"If Jillian wouldn't have a fit, perhaps."

"Who is Jillian?" Dominic asked. "Your mom?"

Waverly nodded and took her seat. "Yes."

"I get it." Dominic nodded and took a seat, as well. "She'd want to be there at our wedding."

"Maybe so," said Waverly. "I think she'd be more pissed off at me ruining my chances to enter the Miss Georgia Pageant next year. A married woman cannot enter."

Dominic nodded slowly while he fixed two slices together like she did. "Okay, so we'll hold off our wedding until after you win."

"No," said Waverly.

"No?" Dominic repeated with a hint of hurt in his deep voice.

"Sorry. It's a habit for me to say I'm running for Miss Georgia." Waverly picked up a slice of her pizza and took a bite of the tip. For a moment she closed her eyes and let her tongue savor the spiciness of the pepperoni and the creamy yet salty flavor of the mozzarella cheese. When she opened her eyes, she found Dominic staring at her.

"I can't eat until you tell me the rest of the story."

"There's nothing much to tell," Waverly said with a shrug. "I was a beauty queen and now I'm…" She hesitated and hated the idea of telling Dominic the whole story—meme and all. "I'm an outcast."

"Outcast means drama-free." Dominic raised his beer in the air. "Here's to being an outcast."

Waverly lifted her beer in cheer. Their bottles clinked in a toast and they ate for a few minutes in silence. There were a few moans of pleasure here and there from the both of them, each enjoying a true American pastime. Halfway through his first slice, Dominic cleared his throat.

"I'm going to assume it's safe to say you know about pageants."

An uncomfortable lull washed over Waverly. She hated having to explain pageant life to people who weren't familiar with the culture. Irresponsible television documentaries made a mockery of the sport. Most folks ironically judged women who donned bathing suits and ball gowns. Waverly did not want Dominic to get the wrong idea of her. "Are you serious?"

Chewing, Dominic shrugged. Distracted, Waverly wondered how much weight he lifted every day to get his muscles so big. The fabric of his cotton shirt was stretched to the limit against his tattooed arms. She couldn't make out all the designs but could identify a bird, maybe an eagle or a hawk, a few knives and words written in a foreign language. Clearly he was addicted to the ink. Sweat beaded above her upper lip and she began to perspire under her arms. Waverly knew summers in Southwood brought a whole new meaning to *Southern heat*, but damn, Dominic Crowne rewrote the definition. She took a swig of her beer.

"I've been out of the country," said Dominic. "I didn't think I missed so much. What's up?"

If he hadn't heard about her embarrassment, it would only be a matter of time. In order to get ahead of the embarrassing meme, she needed to show him now. Waverly pushed away from the counter and retrieved her cell phone. The latest version had been turned into a mock-up video spliced together with images, the work of someone's overactive imagination. The tiara was turned into a silver keg, and instead of Waverly placing the crown on her replacement's head, she was knocking her out. Little cartoon blue and yellow birds flew around her replacement's head.

"Well—" Waverly sighed "—here's what you've missed." Dread washed over her. How long after he watched the video would it be until he keeled over with laughter?

"Hey," Dominic said softly, covering the phone in her hand, "whatever you want to show me, I'm sure it is in the past. I'm interested in you today, here in the present."

"You really need to see this before you get involved with me."

Dominic winked and washed away her fear with the stroke of his fingers against her wrist. "So you admit you're interested in me."

"I don't see how we can marry tonight without a mutual attraction," Waverly said with a grin. She pulled her wrist away, hating the immediate withdrawal of his touch. Addicted after one touch?

Dominic wiped his hand against the length of his face. "Attraction is putting it mildly. We eat the same kind of cupcake and pizza, drink the same beer."

The imaginary neon orange warning sign over his head flashed, but Waverly ignored it. Why bother following the rules now? An unmistakable pull drew her close to him. Her wrist twitched for him to take it again;

he did, and let his fingers lace with hers. "What more proof do we need?"

As if to show her, Dominic rose to his feet and brought his face down, close to hers. His lips lingered over her mouth, his breath teasing her with anticipation. Waverly rose on tiptoe, inciting the kiss, fanning the flames of desire boiling between them. Dominic caressed the side of her face with his free hand. His fingers found their way into her hair and tousled the loose strands. His lips covered hers.

His tongue gracefully entered her mouth, introduced itself to Waverly's and slipped away. Her hand had twitched with withdrawal a few minutes ago, and Waverly's lips quivered when Dominic pulled away for a moment. Not done with their kiss, Dominic turned his head to the other side and cupped both her cheeks. For the first time in weeks, Waverly forgot about everything else in the world. A rumble rolled through her belly. How fast would it make her if she invited Dominic to her bedroom?

"I have my answer," Dominic whispered. He kissed her lips one last time before he pulled away and stood to his full height. "How about you?"

Waverly pressed her forehead against his chest. The beat of his heart sounded against hers. "What was the question?"

Chuckling, Dominic dropped his hands and stepped backward to hold out her seat for her. "We should stop."

"We should," Waverly agreed with a slight shake of her head.

They went back to eating, forgetting how their pizza chilled while the tension between them heated with each bite. Waverly tossed her crust onto the plate. "My God, that was good."

"The pizza or the kiss?"

"The pizza *is* fantastic," Waverly answered with a sly grin. "So tell me, Dominic Crowne, what do you do at this garage of yours?"

After hearing her question out loud, Waverly hated to admit how foolish she sounded. She'd almost taken this man to her bedroom without knowing the first thing about him.

"Well, besides the typical oil changes and routine work on cars," Dominic said, "I restore old cars and customize them for clients."

"What's the last big project you worked on?"

Dominic took a long drink of his beer before answering. "This morning I flew in from Dubai after a two-week trek of bringing my friend Aamir his customized Ferrari."

"What did you do to it?"

"I put in some speakers and tires and fixed the motor so he can maximize the power when he races."

Waverly frowned. "And how old is he?"

"Thirty, like me, almost thirty-one."

"Ah," Waverly drawled, "so he's old."

Dominic nodded. "Oh, you got jokes?"

"I'm known to say something funny a time or two," Waverly told him with a laugh. "So did it take two weeks to deliver a car?"

"Wait until you meet Aamir at our wedding," Dominic said. "You'll understand."

Waverly's heart surged again. She knew he was teasing about the marriage, but hearing someone making plans for something other than beauty pageants felt good…human, almost. Speaking of being human, Waverly reached for a third slice of pizza. "How did you end up with friends overseas?"

"College," he answered. "Stanford, to be exact."

"Oh, that's too interesting." Waverly bit her bottom lip for a half second. Here she was, barely a full semester under her belt with a tarnished tiara, while he was highly educated and worldly. "I hear those Ivy League schools are stuck-up."

"Stanford is not Ivy League," Dominic countered. He held out his muscular arm. "Would a guy tatted like me get into an Ivy League school?"

"How would I know?" Waverly shrugged. "Maybe as a graduation treat, you'd got yourself a few tattoos."

"I promise you, I had tattoos before I started college."

Waverly didn't know why this was an issue. Dominic stood up, reaching for his phone in his back pocket. "Don't try to show me some Photoshopped version of yourself."

"What do you know about Photoshopping?" he asked.

A little too much these days, Waverly thought to herself.

"I say we make a wager of this," Dominic began. "If I can prove you wrong, you have to do something with me."

Considering what they almost did, sure. Waverly grinned. "Deal."

"Don't go back on a promise, now."

Waverly rolled her eyes and held out her hand. "Man, if you don't show me this picture…"

Playfully Dominic held the phone in the air and out of her reach. Now would be the great time for her to come up with her part in the wager when Dominic failed to provide the photograph. Wasn't he the prize, though? Waverly licked her lips in anticipation.

"Bam," Dominic said after his thumb stopped scrolling across the screen. He shoved the phone close to her face.

Waverly took a step backward to adjust what she saw. There, surrounded by a set of twin preteen boys flexing their nonexistent muscles and a young girl, draped in an oversize green graduation gown, was a young Dominic. His hair was cut in a high top fade, too high for his graduation cap, which he held in one hand. He wore a pair of jeans with holes at the knees and a muscle shirt. Dark tattoos covered his biceps. Considering how buff he was now compared to then, Waverly had to concede.

"This is your high school graduation. How old do you have to be to get a tattoo?"

"Sixteen with your parents' approval. My mom came with me," Dominic said. "Ever been around someone with tattoos?"

Waverly sighed. "My first serious boyfriend had them. But since he was older, I assumed."

"Okay," Dominic said, blowing out a sigh in the universal manner of changing the subject. "I've proven you wrong and now it's time to pay up."

Excitement flashed within her. A date? The movies? "Sure," Waverly replied in an even-keeled tone.

Dominic extracted something from the back pocket of his jeans. A folded envelope.

"While I was gone, I got this thing. My sister thinks I need it to fit in with the community better."

"What thing?"

"The Miss Southwood Pageant. Have you heard of it?"

Dread loomed over her. Waverly nodded. "I have."

"Plan on entering?"

The combs of her tiara dug into her scalp as she shook her head. "No. I haven't been in Southwood long enough to have a sponsor."

"Well, that's what I'm saying. I need a beauty queen, and you look like you'd be good at it. You even come with your own crown and everything."

Tuesday morning Dominic woke with a slight hangover, but given what he accomplished last night, he didn't care. He secured himself a beauty queen and managed to pass himself off as a gentleman by not ripping off Waverly's clothes and carrying her to the bedroom. She was so damn irresistible when she tried to back out of the pageant. He saved himself from eating Alisha's idea of a pizza and still got back to his sister's condo in time to feed Hamilton his carrots seconds before Alisha stumbled through the front door at one in the morning. He was in such a good mood, he didn't care if Alisha banged on the guest bedroom door where he slept every time he came over there. The chain dangling from the ceiling fan rattled with each pound of her fist.

"I know you're up." Alisha rattled the door. "You're not snoring."

Damn, with everything he completed before going to bed, Dominic forgot to lock the room. "I don't…" Before he got the words out, Alisha poked her head inside. "Alisha, I could have been naked."

"You better not be naked in my house." Alisha stepped forward and cringed. "Gross."

"What do you want?" Dominic pulled himself up

onto his elbows. Hamilton oinked at Alisha's feet. Today he wore a rainbow tutu.

"Is there anything you want to tell me?" she asked.

"No." Did she figure out he didn't eat her pizza or was barely over here last night?

"Are you sure?"

"Just tell me what's going on, Alisha," Dominic growled. Hamilton, protective of his mother, oinked at him. Would it be wrong of him to eat a slice of bacon in front of the pig?

Alisha crossed her arms and kicked the edge of the bed. "You have a visitor."

"Waverly?"

"Who?" Alisha's upper lip curled. "Jesus, you're back one day and you've got women coming out of the woodwork for you. This one is married, though."

"Lexi," Dominic said with a nod.

"Why is the pageant producer in my living room with a butt load of dresses? Have you decided you're going to change up your wardrobe?" Alisha rambled on while Dominic grabbed his jeans he'd hung over the chair last night and went into the bathroom to change. She was still rattling on about dresses, so like any good big brother, Dominic patted her on the head and headed out of the bedroom and down the hall to greet Lexi Pendergrass Reyes.

Racks of ball gowns filled the living room, covering the messy pigsty Alisha lived in. The front door opened and closed while two men dressed in white smocks rolled in more racks of clothing. Hamilton's feet scrambled down the hall and out the door. Alisha quickly followed but not before shooting an angry glare at her brother. Somewhere in the mix, Lexi's blond head bobbed around. He heard her voice and another woman's as well, but couldn't see who the second person was.

"Good morning?" Dominic said to announce his presence. Lights spilled in from the opened curtains. The doors to the balcony were closed but the clear skies were welcome.

"Dominic," Lexi exclaimed.

Dominic made his way through a row of dresses in every shade of yellow. "What's all this?"

"These—" Lexi waved her arm over the racks "—are all dresses in Waverly's size that are not mine."

Everyone in town, male or female, understood *the* place to buy a dress was at Grits and Glam Gowns. For Alisha, the boutique was one of the bonuses of agreeing to move to Southwood. Lexi made one-of-a-kind dresses for proms, weddings and, most famously, pageants.

"Why wouldn't she get any of your dresses?"

"Conflict of interest," Lexi's assistant answered.

"Sorry, let me make the introductions," said Lexi. "Dominic, this is Kenzie Swayne. She's my right-hand woman for the pageant."

Kenzie, all of five-three, stepped forward and extended her hand for a firm shake. "Pleased to meet you, Mr. Crowne. I've been meaning to stop by your garage. You realize it was once the city jail?"

"I did not," said Dominic. He flexed his hand to revive the circulation. "You'll have to tell me about it."

"Just not today," said Lexi. "I have a limited amount of time."

Dominic glanced down at Lexi's protruding pregnant belly. "How far along are you?"

"Seven months," Lexi said with a shake of her blond head. "But that's not why there's no time. I've got to turn the reins over to Kenzie."

"Because of Waverly?"

"Exactly," Lexi and Kenzie chorused.

Scratching the back of his head, Dominic sighed. "I don't understand. I didn't mean for you to leave your duties as the pageant director, Lexi. I don't understand what the big deal is." He stood uncomfortably as Kenzie gave him a blank stare. After a half second or more, she blinked in disbelief. "What'd I say?" he asked.

Lexi pushed Kenzie playfully on the shoulder. "Kenzie is just in shock to find someone who clearly doesn't know about Waverly Leverve."

Leverve—that's right. She did tell him her last name. Hell, it didn't matter. Like he told Waverly last night, her last name would change soon enough. Dominic squared his shoulders, not sure how to take Kenzie's question. "I know her now."

"Then you know she was stripped of her crown a few weeks ago?" Kenzie asked.

"It was a misunderstanding," Lexi countered. "It wouldn't be ethical for me to stay on board if Waverly is going to enter my contest. Rumors would spread that I fixed it due to our closeness. I used to coach her, you see."

"Like Little League?"

Kenzie scoffed. Her mouth dropped open. "You've seriously never heard of Waverly? The dethroning, the memes?"

"Oh my God, the memes," Lexi reiterated with a shake of her head. "They're getting worse," she said to Kenzie, who nodded.

Maybe that's what Waverly tried to show him last night. Dominic held his hand up. "Look, I've worked on cars my whole life. I can take one look at a piece of metal that's been through the wringer and recreate it as a beautiful piece of art. I don't need to see where Waverly came from. I know what I see now. I don't need any memes."

"Are you comparing Waverly to a hunk of junk?" Kenzie asked.

"Not at all." Dominic chuckled. She was beyond just beautiful. She was captivating and breathtaking. "Whatever happened in her past, I will restore justice."

Lexi offered Dominic a sweet smile, almost motherly. "And for that, I can't be any more grateful, which is why I need to step down, to make sure no one can question Waverly's victorious return to the crown."

While the three of them agreed their main focus was on Waverly, Alisha stood in her doorway, Hamilton in her arms. "Wait, am I to understand you're doing this for someone other than Tiffani?"

"This is for Waverly," Dominic said.

"Who the hell is Waverly?" Alisha asked. Anger filled her cheeks with a red tint. He knew he was in for a cursing out. Dominic glanced up at the dark oak ceiling to avoid her wrath.

"I am."

Alisha turned. Lexi and Kenzie squealed. Without thinking, Dominic's hand clutched his heart when he saw her standing behind Alisha. She wore her hair in a ball at the top of her head, no makeup and a tan turtleneck paired with what looked like a pair of denim overalls. Waverly glared at him with her dark eyes. If looks could kill…

"I've seen you around," Alisha said. "I didn't realize you and my brother were friends."

Waverly blinked and glanced at everyone in the living room. "Apparently your brother has a lot of friends these days. Lexi? Kenzie? What's going on in here?"

"Surprise!" Lexi cheered, followed by Kenzie pumping her fist in the air.

Chapter 3

A sticky, sweet smell of hair spray hugged the air behind the backstage curtains of the Miss Southwood Beauty Pageant, masking the stench of fear as well as envy. Waverly sat in her black swivel chair as her makeup artist, Titus, applied a fresh layer of foundation on her face, hopefully covering the embarrassment of the last five days of pure pageant torment since she'd entered.

The moment Waverly arrived at the Magnolia Palace, where the pageant would take place, she knew Tiffani had abandoned her. Tiffani took one look at her and Waverly knew not to step foot in The Cupcakery for a while. It was clear to Waverly from the beginning that no one appreciated her being there. So much for the friendly Southern hospitality she had grown used to.

On the first day of rehearsals, she'd been accidently

tripped by a girl who claimed to be a virgin stiletto walker. The women Waverly practiced the opening number with told her to go in the wrong direction, so Waverly ended up bumping into everyone when they all gathered together. The dance instructor and director of the pageant talent team at Grits and Glam Studios, Chantal Hairston, took mercy on her and gave Waverly a few pointers—which didn't help the camaraderie from the contestant girls. Waverly tried to remember her cause. For everyone else, this was just a title and a crown to wear around town. For Waverly, this was her last shot at staying on task for her lifelong dream at a shot of becoming Miss Georgia. Pageanting was the only thing she knew how to do.

As the pageant neared its end, at the head of the pack were Tiffani, a girl from the teen division and Waverly. Waverly steadied her breathing. Surprisingly, she made it through the top five—beating the odds stacked against her. Not only did Waverly lack support from the other contestants, but she didn't have any fans with the judges, either. At least not with one. The current Miss South Georgia, Lexi's successor had been a thorn in Waverly's side for as long as she could remember. Before opening Grits and Glam Gowns, Lexi had worked as a private pageant coach for Vera Laing. As children, Waverly and Vera often competed for the same crowns. Waverly always got the win. Waverly blew out the nervousness in the pit of her stomach.

"You all right, *chérie*?" Titus asked. Her makeup artist stood at least six feet five inches tall and towered over her in the chair.

"I'm good," Waverly lied. "How are you doing? I heard a lot is at stake for you."

Titus pressed his lips together, took a step backward and kissed his fingers. "Girl, it's more than just a stake. My job is on the line." He leaned closer, nodded and whispered, "Against that heifer right there."

Ravens Cosmetics, one of the longest-running black-owned cosmetic companies catering to women of color, sponsored the event. This year the executives decided to take the opportunity during the pageant to choose their next employee. Titus and the other makeup artists vied for the creative design director position. Titus's work on Waverly had got her this far. There was one other person giving him competition. The renowned makeup artist Zoe Baldwin worked on Tiffani's touch-up. Titus was equally talented. Waverly just had a penchant for anything eighties and Zoe's makeup brought back a lot of the bright colors. Titus and Waverly looked over at Zoe's station. Tension hung in the air. Thankfully the lights dimmed.

No matter how many pageants, sashes and titles she won, nervousness washed over her. All it took was for someone to not like her dramatic eye makeup or the song she sang or the way her body jiggled after weeks of a steady diet of pizza, beer and cupcakes. Waverly's heart raced. Why did she bother entering? Was she so desperate to get the Miss Georgia crown?

"Next time I see you," said Titus, helping Waverly to her feet, "you'll have the Miss Southwood tiara on your head."

"Thanks for the vote of confidence," Waverly said with a weak smile. She gathered the hem of her buttercup-yellow gown—not designed by Lexi. The deep V-neck might be the reason she lost. In the past she'd won only with a Grits and Glam gown.

Panic set in again. Waverly lined up behind the curtain with Tiffani and the other girl. Surprisingly, Tiffani reached for Waverly's hand and gave it a squeeze. The crowd clapped when they took the stage. Waverly glanced into the crowd out of habit for her mother. Jillian didn't even know she'd entered. Bright lights blinded her. Did Lexi show? Was anyone out there cheering for her?

Consumed with doubt and fear, Waverly moved on autopilot. She smiled and answered her questions. Even though she couldn't see them, Waverly felt Vera's daggers. Knowing the hatred her nemesis had for her motivated Waverly. The judges narrowed their choices, and then there were two—Tiffani and Waverly. Standing close together, Waverly and Tiffani held hands again. She searched the crowd for the spot where she last spotted Dominic. His smile and gentle, encouraging nod calmed her soul.

"No matter what happens," Tiffani whispered, "I am kinda glad to be standing next to you."

Waverly blinked back a threatening tear. "Tiffani, I am really sorry for the way things turned out. I don't want you to think I underhanded you."

"I don't," Tiffani said with a toothy smile. "At least, not anymore. Being up here with you means I am with the best of the best."

"Ladies and gentlemen," the emcee announced into a silver microphone, "it is now time to present to you the second runner-up, Miss Frosting. Congratulations, Tiffani."

The crowd erupted into what Waverly deciphered as cheers. Tiffani hugged Waverly's neck, then stepped backward for Waverly to take her walk to the front of the stage. The former Miss Southwood placed a seven-inch, diamond tiara on top of Waverly's head. *Welcome to the family*, she said silently to the tiara. With her head held high she walked forward on the stage, blowing kisses and mouthing "thank you" to the judges. The triumphant walk refueled her dreams of Miss Georgia.

Titus grabbed Waverly by the hand and swung her around in the air. "We did it!" he cried.

"Thank you so much," said Waverly. She touched just under her right eye to make sure her mascara didn't run.

"It ain't going anywhere—you're wearing Ravens Reign-Proof mascara," Titus reassured her with a wink.

A man in a dark suit approached them with a bright smile across his handsome face. "Ah, a man who knows his products," he said, extending his hand to Titus.

"Waverly, allow me to introduce you to Charles Ravens."

Waverly wasn't sure if she needed to curtsy for the heir to makeup royalty.

"May I say what an honor it is to meet you?" Waverly settled on a handshake.

Mr. Ravens clapped his soft hands over hers. "The honor is all mine, Miss Southwood. You wear our products well."

The tiara tilted when she nodded in appreciation. Mr. Ravens went on to congratulate Titus on his new appointment as creative design director at Ravens Cosmetics. Zoe Baldwin came over and congratulated Waverly. Honor filled Waverly. As the executive spoke with Titus and Zoe, reality sank in for Waverly. All this started from a silly wager over pizza. How different would things be right now, if her original thought of the wager had been a simple kiss? She and Dominic might be in bed together. Rehearsal this week left little time for Dominic. She owed him everything. Dominic reset her track to becoming Miss Georgia. Hell, she still couldn't believe she'd won.

"I knew you'd win." Dominic's deep voice whispered as he stepped up to Waverly, causing a chill down her spine when his large hand wrapped around the curve of her waist. Waverly shifted the dozen roses in her arms and realized another man had come over with Dominic. Dominic made the introductions. "Waverly," he said against her ear, "I want to introduce you to my brother Will Ravens."

"Brother?" Waverly looked back and forth at the two of them. The judge, Will Ravens, was the CEO of Ravens Cosmetics. When Dominic wanted to look sharp in a suit, he definitely looked the part of a business mogul… even standing next to one.

"Frat brother," Dominic explained. "We went to college together."

For some reason it surprised Waverly to learn Dominic joined a fraternity in college. She pictured him as a loner, honing his mechanic skills on his car. But then again, Dominic did say over dinner that he hated being referred to as a mechanic. He was an engineer.

"Yes," said Charles, "Will was one of the judges today."

"That's right." Waverly nodded and recalled the introduction. The contestants had been sequestered in downtown Southwood and kept away from the judges just to lower the odds of fraternization. The judges weren't revealed until the pageant. Turning slightly to her side, Waverly came face-to-face with Dominic with the help of her four-inch strappy sandals. Dominic pressed his lips against her temple. A warm and fuzzy feeling washed over her.

Photographers shoved cameras in her face. Flashes blinded her. People stood by her side, wanting photograph after photograph. All the shame she'd gone through by losing the Miss South Georgia title washed away. She tried to focus on the main goal—the road to Miss Georgia—but the only thing on her mind was the secure hold Dominic kept around her waist as he stood next to her.

Zoe Baldwin and Will Ravens appeared together. "Pleased to meet you, Waverly. Congratulations on your win."

"Thank you," Waverly said slowly. Waverly stepped forward and shook Zoe's hand. "You're awesome, Miss Zoe. It was a real pleasure to meet you this afternoon. I am a huge fan."

"But better working with me." Titus brought up the rear of the group. His smugness was enough to knock Zoe off the stage with a quick hip bump. Waverly frowned at the action.

But any time she had to be alone, she wanted to spend with Dominic. She wanted to properly thank him for the dress he had flown in from Italy.

"I thought we could go out and celebrate tonight," Dominic said with a hug.

"Sounds good to me." Waverly inhaled his scent, committing it to memory. He smelled spicy.

"I know we haven't spent any time together this week due to practicing for the pageant, and I am looking forward to spending more time alone with you," Dominic began. "Will's leaving in the morning and I wanted to include him tonight for dinner."

The pit of her stomach dropped. Waverly prayed she covered her disappointment with a wide, toothy smile. "Sure."

Another reporter came over, this one from *Pageant Pride Gazette*, wanting a few words. Running in the same circles as her, Waverly had come across Marion Strickland several times before, and she knew this interview was important, especially if she was ever going to shake the dethroning incident.

Waverly reluctantly left Dominic's side to take care of pageant business besides winning a ton of products from Ravens Cosmetics and a chance to apply for the Miss Georgia. Waverly's heart swelled with pride. She hadn't even told her mother about trying out for another pageant. This one she'd accomplished without her mother's help. And it felt good.

For a better background, the reporter and her cameraman suggested filming the interview outside on the docks of Magnolia Palace. Dominic and his friend moseyed outside, as well. From across the lush, green yard, Dominic nodded in her direction. They both caught each other at the right time. He stood listening to his friend and winked. Dominic's smile made her toes curl. What a shame they were going to share dinner tonight with his friends, Waverly thought. Maybe for dessert she'd find another way to thank Dominic for his help. A burning desire to run her hands underneath his jacket consumed her. From being around him, she'd memorized every inch of his body. It was time to commit the feel of his body, as well.

"Here we are again, Miss Waverly," said Marion. "Or shall I now call you Miss Southwood?" They both sat on wooden benches on the docks of the Magnolia Palace, overlooking the private lake. The high afternoon sun sent sparkles from her diamond tiara, which were reflected across Marion's face.

"Come on now, Marion," Waverly gushed. "We go back a while now. You can just call me Waverly."

Marion, a gorgeous young woman close to thirty, smiled. "So you know I'm curious about the whole incident leading up to being dethroned."

Of course she was, Waverly thought. "Must we?" she asked with a droll sigh. "The incident is a thing of the past." Thanks to her fast track into the Miss Southwood Pageant, Waverly had never had a chance to tell Dominic the full story surrounding her being dethroned.

"I understand," said Marion. "I guess we can tell everyone you're back on track. It is nice to see you bounce back so quickly."

"Thank you," Waverly said, reaching out and squeezing Marion's hand.

"Well, I won't hold you up. I just wanted to get a few pictures of you outside with your gorgeous tiara."

Perfect timing, Waverly thought as Dominic made his way toward her. His hands stretched out for Waverly to take. "Almost done here?"

"Almost, stud," Marion answered.

"It turns out Will and Zoe can't make it tonight. Are you okay if it's just us?"

"Just us?" Marion asked, stepping between the two of them. "And exactly who are you to Waverly?" Before letting either one of them give an answer, Marion walked around Dominic's large frame. "Let's see, I feel like I'm sensing more than a sponsorship. You're dressed in a five-thousand-dollar suit. You smell of money and success. So you're not Waverly's typical bad boy."

Waverly bit her bottom lip and glanced toward the water to avoid Dominic's questioning yet curious gaze.

Dominic let the reporter's comment go and headed off to let them finish their conversation. Waverly's past was just that—the past. They were here in the present together. Just as each time he restored a job to its fullest potential, pride washed over him. A tiara belonged on Waverly's head. She had the wave down pat, too. But a part of Dominic understood her project wasn't complete. The next big step for her was the Miss Georgia competition. He looked forward to helping her out until then. Once she moved on to the next level, his job was done. Dominic understood how this worked. While restoring cars, he often thought of them as his until the time came to turn over the keys to the rightful owner. He'd be able to do the same with Waverly, right? Just walk away.

Hell, the erotic tension between them had held him over for the week. Tuesday morning Lexi allowed him to stay at his sister's place while Waverly sorted through Lexi's choices of gowns. Not only did they let him stay, they asked for his opinion. Dominic wasn't sure if it was the actual dress he loved on Waverly or the near orgasmic feeling he'd got when he helped her zip the dress up and down. A long whistle snapped him out of his daydream. He found himself face-to-face with his frat brother.

A slick smile spread across Will's face. "I can't wait for you to find the woman who makes you drop everything for her."

Dominic glanced over at Waverly. She waved again. Her smile melted his insides. With a straight face, he shrugged and turned his attention back to his frat brother. They'd been through the trenches together. Will was more than a frat brother; they were real brothers.

Like a sibling would, Will punched Dominic in the biceps. "Ouch." Will winced.

"Sitting behind your cushy desk has made you soft," said Dominic.

"You moving to the country has made you soft." Will pointed toward Waverly. "Be careful with that one."

Dominic held his hand up. "Wait a minute, now."

"Hold on, big fellow." Will held up his hands in the air in surrender. "Don't get me wrong, I like the idea of you getting involved with someone—hell, it's about time."

"You're one to talk." Dominic chuckled uncomfortably. He didn't need to be reminded about his bachelorhood. Oh, there'd been plenty of women. Tons of casual flings. But so far he avoided relationships with women by focusing on his business. He prided himself on not stringing them along. He never wanted to be like his father.

"Right, but I'm selective with who I pick. I don't know when the last time you dated anyone was, and trying to date a beauty queen, well…"

"Because you've dated so many?" Dominic asked his frat brother.

"No." Will shook his head. "But I was a judge on a panel with a few beauty queens. Their schedules are demanding and sometimes they have to break promises."

"So?"

"So?" Will mocked him. "I know how you feel about broken promises and living drama-free. And I don't want you to go into any relationship with the new Miss Southwood blind. She's going to be busy."

"Fine by me." Dominic inhaled the evening air. "I moved to Southwood for my business, not for love."

"All right." Will sighed. "I trust you know what you're doing."

The fact he was standing off to the side, waiting for Waverly to finish, when he needed to work in the garage already told Dominic he didn't know what he was doing. Whatever it was, it felt good. Dominic's heart swelled with excitement when Waverly made her way toward the two of them. Deep down he'd known Waverly would win. She dazzled the crowd just as she dazzled him. They hadn't spent a lot of time together this week, but the kiss they'd shared offered so much promise. Dominic's body rippled with desire. He needed her. The fact his body reacted so strongly toward her worried Dominic. Neither of them were in the position to commit to anything serious and while it seemed like the perfect situation for a relationship-leery man, it left Dominic feeling unsettled.

"Mr. Ravens," Waverly said with a genuine smile. "I have one more meeting, with the mayor, a brief one, and then we can head off to dinner."

Will leaned forward and gave Waverly a kiss on her cheek. "If Zoe and I will be in Miami tonight but the next time we're in the same city we'll have to get together. I just wanted to stop by and offer my congratulations again and say bye to this lug right here."

Dominic ducked out of the way when Will tried to wrap his arm around his neck. "Man."

"He was never a cooperative line brother," Will explained to Waverly.

Waverly's lips pressed together. Dimples formed in

her cheeks as she tried not to grin too hard. "I can imagine."

"Will?"

The three of them standing there on the docks turned toward the voice. Vera, one of the other judges who sat on the panel, came barreling toward them. Anson Wilson, the town's mayor, followed close behind. Dominic had met the politician when he first moved to Southwood. The man wore a designer scarf at all times. Alisha once explained to Dominic it was an ascot. Dominic privately called him Mayor Ascot. The man was somewhere in his thirties, clearly a former football star at Southwood High School. Every time Dominic saw the man away from the office he had some form of high school football paraphernalia on, alluding to the old days.

"Oh, Will, there you are. I came to give you your score sheets," Vera said.

Dominic glanced at the tallies. He couldn't help noticing all the check marks in Waverly's favor. Dominic wrapped his arm around Will's neck and put him in a playful headlock. "That's my boy."

"Uh, thanks, Vera," Will said as he pulled away from Dominic's grip. He took the paper, folded it up and tucked it into the inside pocket of his jacket, hiding it, almost. "Well, I better get going."

"Something I said?" asked Vera.

"You have a funny knack for clearing a room," said Waverly.

Dominic's brows rose. He hated drama, especially between women. Tension filled the gorgeous evening. The mayor felt it and cleared his throat.

"No need for things to get testy, ladies," said Anson.

Since the day Dominic opened shop, he had liked the man.

"Hold up a minute," Dominic said, trying to control his bubbling irritation. He didn't like the idea of anyone trying to scold Waverly, especially when this Vera lady came over here with her antagonizing tone. Will stepped forward, placing himself between the local politician and Dominic's wrath.

"Mayor." Will intervened. "Thank you for allowing Ravens Cosmetics to come to your lovely city."

Distracted, Anson beamed. "The pleasure is all mine."

"I was just coming to find you," Waverly said to him, which irked Dominic, especially with the goofy smile on Mayor Ascot's face. The idea of her going to any other man didn't sit right with him.

"We actually came to find the both of you," said Anson, looking at Dominic and Waverly.

"You were?" Waverly and Dominic chorused.

"Yes." Anson nodded. "Vera pointed out the morality clause in our Miss Southwood contract."

"What the hell are you…?"

Waverly placed her hand on Dominic's forearm. He calmed down immediately. Will leaned forward and raised his brows at the position of Waverly's hand. She held a power over Dominic, one Will now knew Dominic could not control. "It's standard in every pageant."

"We just want to make sure things are fair," Vera said sweetly.

"We?" Waverly scoffed.

Vera stepped close to Anson, linking her arm through his. The way Anson looked at Waverly versus the way he cringed at Vera's intimate touch clued

Dominic in on everything he needed to know about the mayor.

"The mayor doesn't want or need a scandal brought down on his city," Vera went on. "And we all know how scandal follows you around, don't we, Waverly?"

Waverly dug her nails into Dominic's skin. He wondered what they'd feel like against his back while he made love to her. The woman had physical power.

"I am well aware of the morality clause, *Vera*," Waverly bit out. "I plan on holding this title with the utmost respect."

"Good. So just to make sure, the relationship between the two of you—" Vera wagged her finger between Dominic and Waverly "—is professional?"

Waverly's shoulders squared.

"What business of yours is it if we're professional or not?" Dominic asked.

Vera's high-pitched laughter pierced Dominic's ears. "Don't you think the pageant board will find it convenient that Waverly's sponsor had his best friend participating as a judge? Talk about calling in favors. Sounds like an ethics violation to me."

"Now, hold on one damn minute," said Will. "I didn't know Dominic sponsored anyone."

"Of course you didn't," Vera said condescendingly. For extra oomph she nodded with her eyes widened. Vera dramatically pressed her hand over her heart. "*I* believe you."

"Look," Anson said, then cleared his throat. "I know we just met a few weeks ago, Waverly, but I will believe anything you say. Tell us there's nothing going on between you and him to give us a reason why Will's vote might have been influenced. A lot of time and money went into this pageant. People will be unhappy if they found out this was rigged."

Waverly took a step away from Dominic's side. His heart ached but he didn't know why. In truth, other than a kiss, nothing had happened between them. If only he hadn't made that wager over whether or not he had a picture of himself tattooed at graduation.

"We're just friends," Waverly said with a shake of her head.

The words couldn't have hurt any worse if she had stabbed him in the heart.

"Good," Anson said with a bounce. He turned to Waverly. "I look forward to seeing you on the Christmas Advisory Council this week."

"The what?" Waverly shook her head.

"The Christmas Advisory Council," repeated Anson. "The big bonus of being Miss Southwood is the countdown to Christmas. Believe it or not, we start in the summer to get things ready for the big Christmas parade. As the mayor of Southwood, I will be spending a lot of time with you. We will end Christmas passing out presents together, kind of like Mr. and Mrs. Claus. I look forward to serving with you."

Dominic wasn't completely sure Anson had said the word *with*. It sounded more like *serving you*. The three-foot gap between the mayor and Waverly was far too small for Dominic's preference. And Dominic would be damned if he let Anson nuzzle close to Waverly during this stupid time period.

"We," Dominic said, draping his arm around Waverly's shoulder, "look forward to it."

"We?" Anson, Vera and Will said in unison.

"Sure. I'm a business owner in town." Dominic

winked. "And I am sponsoring the reigning Miss South-wood. We look forward to serving together, don't we, Waverly?"

Waverly gulped. "Yes, sure. Of course."

Bristling, the mayor breathed deeply through his thinly pinched nose. Vera tightened her grip on the straps of her purse. It was so easy getting underneath the mayor's skin. The hardest part was still ahead of Dominic. How was he supposed to continue a platonic relationship after being teased with a kiss from her sweet lips one week ago?

Once Anson and Vera left, Will said goodbye. Waverly and Dominic were left alone. The setting sun haloed her curvy frame. Dominic exhaled.

"How serious are these morality mobs?" he asked, stepping forward.

"Considering I lost my previous title for—" Waverly started to explain and bit her bottom lip as if searching for the right words "—creatively expressing my suggestions to a journalist, I'd say pretty serious."

Frustration—sexual frustration, to be exact—consumed Dominic enough to clench his fists. Waverly's eyes darted downward to his side. Then she took a step backward. For a moment he caught a glimpse of her shoulders shaking. Immediately he regretted not staying in control. He rubbed his hand against the back of his head.

"Sorry." Waverly cringed. "I've got really bad timing."

"This is my fault." Dominic closed the gap between them and reached for her hand. The rough pads of his fingertips traced circles over the small bones of her wrists. "I talked you into running."

"I didn't exactly fight you over the offer," Waverly

said jokingly. Her half smile and shrug made him chuckle.

"No, you didn't."

Waverly gasped playfully and attempted to snatch her hand away, but Dominic closed his hand tighter and drew her against his frame. With their bodies so close, their laughter subsided. Waverly stopped laughing but her pink lips parted. Dominic cleared his throat. It took every ounce of his control to pull away. "We don't want to have the morality mob after us."

"I really am sorry," Waverly repeated and bit her bottom lip. "Do you still want to go to dinner?"

"Hell yeah. If I can't have you anytime soon, the least I can do is spend as much time with you as possible."

"Thank you."

"Don't thank me." Dominic leaned close and whispered in her ear, "I understand why there's a clause."

"Why?"

"Because what I want to do to you is completely immoral."

Chapter 4

Reservations at Duvernay's, one of Southwood's finest restaurants, were made months in advance, even for a weekday. Tonight was no different. Cars filled the parking lot, more than likely owned by people from the pageant and the people in town. The valets were hopping, passing and returning keys. Men and women filled the inside lobby and waited to be seated while some sipped drinks.

Instead of watching Dominic try to slip a hundred-dollar bill to the frazzled teenage hostess who seemed clueless what to do with it, Waverly stepped forward and cleared her throat. The young girl's eyes widened and immediately she recalled an available table. Holding the Miss Southwood title came with perks. Of course, the downside meant Waverly had to curb any feelings she had for Dominic, but this was perfect. No relationship meant more time to focus on her goals: winning Miss Georgia and going on to become Miss USA.

"You didn't have to do that," Dominic said, pulling Waverly's chair out for her.

"I'm sorry," said Waverly over her shoulder. Dominic's lips were an inch from the tip of her ear. She closed her eyes and pushed out the threatening twitch by clearing her throat. "You were about to overwhelm that poor girl with cash. Kids these days love gift cards—cash is obsolete."

"Whatever. Money is money," Dominic grumbled as he moved to his side of the table covered in a white linen cloth. A single candle stood between the two of them. The flickering light highlighted the golden color of his cheeks and the coppery tint of his hair. When she first met him his hair was slightly longer. Dominic smoothed down his paisley tie. The yellow background of his tie matched the color of the dress given to her by Lexi. Did he coordinate with her on purpose? It would be like Lexi to offer such a matching selection. Waverly bit the inside of her cheek to keep from grinning. "Had that been my sister, she would have figured out what to do with the cash"

"Well, I apologize if I hurt your male ego."

"It's fine," Dominic said with a deep exhale.

"Now, back to your sister, Alisha," Waverly began and waited for Dominic's slight nod to confirm she had the name right. "How is she? I didn't see her at the pageant."

"She was there," said Dominic. "She went to meet up with Tiffani after her loss."

"Runner-up isn't a loss." Waverly shrugged and sat back to allow their waiter to pour a glass of water for each of them. She thanked the young man and continued the conversation, leaning forward again to speak in a hushed tone. "You do recall Vera reminding me of my flaws."

Dominic shook his head. "I don't care what that woman said or what it was about, and neither should you."

Waverly waved off his pep talk. "Normally I pay no attention to anything Vera has to say, but you have to agree with what she pointed out."

"What?" he asked.

"You don't think it's a coincidence your best friend…"

"Brother," Dominic corrected her. The smile disappeared for a moment. So, blood or not, Waverly understood Will was family to him.

Waverly nodded. "Brother. Your brother participated as a judge in a pageant I won."

"So? Are you arguing about the legitimacy of your win?"

With the amount of pressure she used to keep her lips from spreading into a goofy grin, Waverly worried her Pageant Pink lipstick from Ravens Cosmetics would smear. "I don't know."

"Correct me if I'm wrong," Dominic said, reaching across the table. He pulled her hand into his and traced a circle around the top of her wrist. He'd done the same move earlier at the docks at the Magnolia Palace and it was just as intoxicating. "You were in a beauty pageant, emphasis on *beauty*."

"Yes," Waverly said with a short nod. Something told her to pull her hand away. People at nearby tables and passing by watched the public display of affection.

"I've never heard of a woman arguing about her beauty."

"Not beauty," said Waverly. "I meant about the contest being rigged."

"Rigged? I thought the point of a pageant was who is the prettiest." Dominic shook his head and pulled his hand away.

She wished then she'd done it first. At least if she moved her hand away, she would be able to control the void she felt from the absence of his touch. Waverly needed to put some distance between them. "We're more than pretty faces," she said of his assessment.

"I didn't mean it as an insult," said Dominic.

"I don't think you understand what I've gone through to get on the Miss Georgia path. I can't have it crash down because of some scandal coming out that Will did a favor for you."

"Like I told the crazy lady," Dominic went on, "I didn't know Will planned on picking you. I knew he came to town on business for Ravens Cosmetics and the pageant, but at the time of his arrival, I hadn't even met you."

Waverly pressed her lips together again. "Okay. Maybe I'll give you the benefit of the doubt."

"Aren't you generous?"

"You are, actually," she said. "Since you're my sponsor, I'm still going to wear your Miss Crowne's Garage sash across my body."

"You can wear anything of mine you like—my sash, this shirt…in the morning after we wake up."

Waverly cleared her throat. "Dominic."

"Waverly."

The waiter came over and took their orders. She

didn't know why she was surprised Dominic ordered a rare steak. Even in his suit, his behavior struck her as primal. Earlier it had been the way he approached her, claiming her with his tone and securing his stance when he held her hand. A shallow breath caught in her throat with the fantasy image of his large hands roaming over her body. Waverly reached for her glass of ice water and took a long drink in an attempt to douse the flame threatening her insides.

Dominic chuckled. "You okay?"

"Yes, I'm fine." Waverly hoped her he believed her lie. "So tell me what you thought of the pageant as a whole."

"Ridiculous."

Heart sinking, Waverly resisted gaping. A warmth of embarrassment touched her cheeks. Dominic did not respect her. She felt silly for putting too much faith in thinking he understood her life. His perception was exactly why Waverly hated letting outsiders into her life. "You'd rather tinker with cars?"

"Cars, I understand." Dominic reached for his glass of water and gulped it halfway down. "Don't get me wrong—you were the prettiest by far—but at least when I restore a vehicle that brings in a hefty commission, the other cars' self-esteems don't deflate and they are not dramatic and catty."

"Uh—" Waverly paused "—Alisha told me you have a desk made out of half a car. That's not dramatic?"

Dominic shook his head no. "Because of a woman. See? Dramatic. You can't have high emotions and expensive cars around."

"Makes sense," Waverly said with a shrug.

"You'll see more when I take you around town."

"I beg your pardon?" Waverly leaned closer to hear better.

"Since I'm sponsoring you in this pageant and you're representing the Crowne name, what better way to reiterate that than by arriving at all your functions in one of my restored vehicles?"

Waverly's eyes narrowed on his large frame. Her lip curled with the idea of being a hood ornament. "Ugh," she moaned with an eye roll. "Why do I get the feeling you're benefiting from this pageant bet we made?"

"I'm always three steps ahead, sweetheart." Dominic winked. The simple gesture spread fire in the pit of her belly.

"We can't…" Her words trailed off; she was hating herself for dampening the moment. Waverly's eyes darted around, as she was half expecting to find the other patrons of Duvernay's staring at them. No one paid them any attention. But still not wanting to risk her chance at the Miss Georgia title, Waverly leaned close. "We can't allow anything to go any further than what happened the other night."

Dominic sat back in his seat. His beefy right hand covered his heart. "What kind of man do you take me for?" he teased with a lopsided grin. "I'm kidding. Waverly, I respect your goals. Your morality clause doesn't mean I can't still help you. I promise I will control myself. The question is, can you?"

An imaginary angel appeared on Waverly's right shoulder, wearing a sparkly tiara and offering Waverly a pageant wave. On the other shoulder, a red version of herself appeared, shooing Waverly off with the back of her hand while an imaginary devil image of Dominic dipped her back for a deep kiss.

Waverly blinked back into focus. "Um, sure, of course I can."

In a matter of eight weeks after being dethroned, Waverly found herself comfortable as the new Miss Southwood. She already visited the senior citizen centers for Southwood and the surrounding cities of Peachville, Black Wolf Creek and Samaritan. Anson, the mayor of Southwood, was kind enough to send a car for Waverly's travels, as well as stay in attendance with her, though she could have walked. She needed to walk. Though the days of drowning her sorrows in cupcakes and pizza were over, they had taken their toll on her curvy frame. Thank God for the slow pageant wave; otherwise her underarms would jiggle.

Waverly arrived at city hall's meeting room for the Christmas Advisory Council meeting. She wore her Miss Southwood tiara and sash over her pearl gray A-line dress. Unlike the other places she'd visited, like the elementary schools and nearby restaurants, no one here seemed to care for her presence. Four dozen chairs split the room in two rows. A wooden podium stood at the front and in the center. Tiptoeing in her pearl gray stilettos, Waverly found a seat by herself toward the back. Other people turned to greet her, but considering how new she was to Southwood, she didn't have the same connection as some of the other ladies gathered in groups, exchanging recipes and secrets. The few minutes she planned to leave early would give her the chance to walk through town and be alone with her thoughts. Before heading inside city hall, she glanced down the street toward Crowne's Garage. The shop closed early and Waverly hoped she'd see Dominic at the meeting. After the pageant he'd made a point to Anson about participating.

Waverly kept her head down and focused on today's agenda. Christmas seemed so far away. Lexi's name popped out at the top of the page with the announcement of the Christmas pageant. Lexi had proposed a plan to open her studios for the children who wanted to participate, clients or not. Waverly made a mental note to make sure she offered her help. Lexi would have her hands full with the baby over the holidays.

Sad, Waverly sighed. This would be the first year she wouldn't be with her parents at Christmas. She hadn't even spoken to her mother about winning Miss Southwood. Jillian managed to avoid the topic of pageants, probably still ashamed to have a dethroned daughter. Waverly wanted to wait until she secured her place on the platform for Miss Georgia before getting her mother's hopes up again.

The sound of metal clanged as people opened the oversize door. Each time, the group of ladies in front of Waverly would glance up and then return to their conversations. On one occasion, the ladies glanced up but then elbowed each other. Waverly adjusted herself in her seat, sitting upright and moving forward to watch their reactions. One woman in a leopard-print dress and pink belt licked her glossy lips. Another woman in all gray fluffed her natural curls, while a third woman sucked in her stomach and arched her back.

Without a doubt, *Dominic was there*.

Only that man's sexual prowess could turn ordinarily smart-looking women into a gaggle of giggling girls. But as the thrill of excitement set in, it was accompanied by a visible set of goose bumps. Waverly knew she wasn't immune.

Waverly bit the insides of her cheeks to keep from grinning. Thank God her will stayed strong and she resisted the urge to turn around.

"Hey," Dominic said.

He found her. Waverly glanced upward. Tonight Dominic wore a pair of khaki chinos and a green striped polo that complemented his light eyes. For a second she was transported back to her freshman dance when her boarding school had invited students from the military academy. No one danced the first few songs until the popular cadet Howard Gilmore, who was known for dating local girls and getting into fights, came over and asked her to dance. She was the belle of the ball. At least now, in this dank conference room, Waverly was the envy of the others. The women in the front stared at her with their lips curled.

Heat from his closeness warmed her shoulder. Waverly blinked several times, feigning that she didn't recognize him. "Hello?"

With a tight-lipped smile, Dominic nodded and took the empty seat beside her. "Funny."

Continuing her charade, Waverly extended her hand. "Have we met? I'm Waverly Leverve. What brings you to this Christmas Advisory Council meeting?"

"Not funny, Waverly," said Dominic. "I promised you I'd be here."

"And you always keep your promises," Waverly mocked. She tried to understand Dominic still had a business to run, but she swore every time he couldn't make an appearance with her, Anson came through, and spending time with the mayor was not something Waverly looked forward to.

"Damn straight," Dominic huffed with a wink. "What'd I miss?"

"Nothing," said Waverly. "I just got here myself."

"What? Mr. Mayor didn't accompany you?" Dominic leaned forward and looked around her at the empty seat. "Where is he hiding?"

Waverly elbowed Dominic in the ribs. Okay, so maybe she wasn't the only one to notice. "Don't be mad at Anson for showing me around. It's not like you've been knocking on my door."

"You wouldn't know." Dominic chuckled. "You've been away from your apartment."

There was some truth to his words, but Waverly refused to cave so quickly. She gave Dominic a once-over, staring him up and down. "Stalker."

"It's only stalking if the other person doesn't know you're after them."

At a loss for words at his irrational logic, Waverly smiled. "Okay, whatever. How have you been?"

"I am better now."

"Busy at the shop?"

The corners of his lips turned down as he thought about his answer. Dominic nodded and rubbed the edges of his goatee. "Busy, but busy is good. I've got a Ford Model K in the shop right now."

"Ah," Waverly said with a nod. "Mr. Myers found you."

"Well, look who is getting to know the townspeople," Dominic said.

"Mr. Myers is a friendly old man," Waverly informed him. "The ladies at the Southwood Elderly Care Community Center are crazy for him. You should see the way they gather at the window when he pulls up in his fancy car."

Dominic nodded. "I imagine it must be like how I've been this week, waiting for you to stop by."

"Anyway." Waverly cleared her throat. What would people think if she just showed up at the garage? She didn't even own a car. People might believe as Miss Crowne's Garage she had work, but Waverly did not want anyone to guess the need she felt to see him. The pageant came first and alone time with Dominic threatened her goals. Given the fever pitch nature of her dreams over the last few nights, maybe it was best Dominic didn't accompany her to events.

"Stalker level?" Dominic asked.

As Waverly nodded, she caught a glimpse of the ladies in front staring at them. "Don't look now but you are gathering a following like Mr. Myers."

Dominic followed Waverly's gaze, then shrugged. "I'll pass. I don't deal well with drama, and they scream it. Besides, I only have eyes for you."

Not sure what to make of him, Waverly pressed her lips together and looked away. She recognized the stares, the eye rolls and the sighs in her direction. The woman in leopard was not a fan of Waverly's. Waverly never thought she'd be glad to see Anson stroll into the room. The mayor commanded the podium, but when he laid eyes on Waverly he smiled kindly. That expression left at the sight of Dominic. Anson pounded his gavel against the wood.

"All right, may I have everyone's attention?" Anson's voice boomed across the conference room. A silver microphone poked out of the top of the podium, but Anson didn't need it. "With this being the first meeting to kick off the start of the Christmas Countdown, we have no old business to take care of."

"Excuse me."

Waverly, along with everyone else in the room, turned in their seats. Kenzie Swayne, Lexi's pageant replacement as director, came forward from the back of the room. Anson grimaced and Waverly smirked. The five-foot-three-inch former cheerleader dominated the attention of the room.

"Kenzie," Anson said, acknowledging her with a nod.

"Thanks for inviting me up here," said Kenzie, grabbing the microphone.

"Well, I didn't but..." Anson's voice trailed off when he realized the mic was on. "To what do we owe the pleasure?"

"As you all know, I am Southwood's only historian and I wanted to make this committee aware that this year, Southwood will celebrate 150 years as an established city."

The crowed oohed and aahed at Kenzie's declaration. Kenzie nodded. "I know. Impressive, right? I wanted to put a bug in y'all's ears about keeping our birthday in your minds for this year's Christmas parade."

A hundred fifty years was a long time, Waverly thought to herself. Each time she earned a new tiara, she was crowned by the two previous winners. At some pageants, she'd even had the first Miss Whatever crown her. Once she stood onstage with at least five generations of beauty queens and the titanic screen behind her flashed images of their gowns behind her. And that had been just fifty years; she wondered what a hundred more years of pageant queens would look like. It meant everything to be a part of history. She wanted to help build the confidence of younger generations.

Anson stepped forward and took the microphone from Kenzie's hands. "And speaking of our Christmas parade, we'll have our very own Miss Southwood in attendance."

Heat prickled Waverly's cheeks when Anson motioned for her to stand. She did and gave everyone a pageant wave. "I wasn't expecting an introduction."

"Don't be silly—everyone needs to know you," Anson went on. "In case any of you missed the crowning on Sunday, Miss Waverly Leverve is our new Miss Southwood and will be our guest judge at all of our town events, like the fair's big pie-eating contest at the pumpkin patch, and cut the ribbon at all the grand openings, as well as my right-hand lady for the Christmas parade. Now, are we ready to get on with business?"

Whether anyone was ready or not, Anson slammed his gavel back on the podium. Dominic leaned over to Waverly and whispered, "One guess what Mayor Ascot wants for Christmas. Or should I say who he wants."

"Will you be quiet?" Waverly said between her teeth.

Dominic settled back in his chair. In a deep stretch, Dominic extended his muscular arms to either side of him and rested it on the back of Waverly's metal chair.

"L-leading up to the, uh," Anson said, verbally stumbling at the podium. He cast his eyes to the back row, exactly where Dominic's arm rested. Out of the corner of her eye she swore she saw Dominic give Anson a thumbs-up. Seemingly in order to gather his thoughts, Anson reached for the pitcher of water and the glass on the table behind him.

"While Mayor Anson is pulling himself together—" Kenzie stepped up again "—have any of you had time to think about a theme for the parade?"

"Oh my God," someone yelled in a joking tone. A few people giggled.

Kenzie brushed off the taunt with a shake of her curly hair. "Surely something has come to mind?"

Crickets. Waverly wished she were quick thinking on her feet, or at least confident enough to speak in front of everyone. She chewed on her bottom lip and summoned the courage to stand. Dominic crossed his arms over his chest and leaned to the side, amusement spread across his face. Kenzie beamed.

"Miss Southwood, do you have an idea?"

Considering Kenzie helped Waverly squeeze into a few dresses last week, there was no need for formality, but Waverly understood.

"Well—" Waverly inhaled "—when you mentioned how old Southwood will be, I thought about all of the pageants I've won over the years."

"Modest, isn't she?" the woman dressed in leopard said loud enough for Waverly to hear. The ladies with her giggled.

Wearing a bikini or a slinky one-piece, teetering on stilettos or answering questions drawn randomly out of a fishbowl didn't faze her, but saying this scared her. The room was so small compared to the stage where the overhead lights blocked the prying eyes of the public. "Okay, well, I was thinking the floats could represent the decades past."

"Brilliant." Kenzie fist-pumped her.

"Absolutely." Anson found his voice again. Once

everyone realized the mayor had Waverly's vote, they all cheered.

Dominic reached over and shook Waverly's hand, never letting go. Tingles consumed her body. Waverly tried to tell herself taking his hand was platonic. "Great idea," he whispered when she sat back down.

"And who did you bring with you tonight?" Kenzie asked Waverly, drawing attention to the two of them. "Who's that seated next to you?"

Waverly pressed her lips together and shook her head at her friend's faux amnesia. She knew exactly who Dominic was.

"She didn't bring anyone," Anson answered with a hint of panic in his voice.

"Hi, Kenzie," Dominic said, lifting his chin in acknowledgment.

"Just the man we could use for the job," said Kenzie.

"Excuse me?" Anson and Dominic chorused as other people asked what kind of job it was.

A breeze filled the room as everyone's heads, from the front of the room to the back, bobbed. Waverly bit her lip and looked up at the lights. A group of the committee started whispering insinuations and jokes. Jesus, she thought to herself. The last thing she wanted was another scandal to jeopardize her dream. She just got this title. She could see the memes now: the Miss Georgia crown dangling in front of her like a carrot.

"Will you stop?" Waverly mouthed to Dominic.

"I didn't do anything," Dominic defended himself.

"Dominic," Kenzie said with a giggle, "I apologize for putting you on the spot. Most of us have seen your Crowne's Garage logo on the back of our Little League team shirts, but not a lot of us have met you. Would you mind standing?"

Dominic rose as asked. Waverly couldn't help but keep her eye line at his tight butt in his chinos. She pressed her lips together and let her eyes trail down to the definition of his thigh muscles, where the fabric pressed against his legs. She bet he looked good in a pair of boxer briefs.

"I understand Mr. Myers is trusting you with his car," Kenzie went on. "I would like to ask everyone in this room that if your car or your grandparents' old car needs fixing, to set up an appointment with Dominic to fix it, because I am going to ask everyone with an old-timey car to participate in pulling the floats. We can use the cars of the decades, too, right, Waverly?"

Eyes widened. Waverly shrugged. "Sounds great to me."

"Well, great." Kenzie beamed again. "And now the more I think about it, the more I realize the two of you could work together, gathering up some old outfits."

"Wait, what?" Waverly asked.

"I can think of a dozen people around Southwood who have a wardrobe filled with vintage clothes from the sixties. I bet seeing you riding around in one of Mr. Crowne's restored antique cars from that era will spark up their memories of what they used to wear back in the day. Maybe they'll want to schlep through their attics for some cute outfits the kids can wear on the parade floats."

Beside her, Dominic brushed his leg against hers. "Sounds like a great plan to me."

Great, Waverly thought. She and Dominic in close quarters. How was she supposed to follow her morality clause?

Chapter 5

As Miss Southwood, Waverly's schedule was hectic and busy to say the least. Her summer of reign dipped into the fall schedule. Waverly and Dominic made appearances in various surrounding counties. She kicked off fairs, cut the ribbon for several restaurant and business openings and judged events at surrounding county fairs, from pig races when there was a tie, to small beauty pageants. A lot of these brought some of the other Southern pageant queens to the stage. With everyone vying to enter the Miss Georgia competition, things became testy. Waverly witnessed a few elbows and slight hip bumps that had made another beauty queen stumble; a few had fallen off a shared stage. The pageant world was becoming a contact sport and social media captured every slip and fall, and added them to the epic-fail category.

Thank goodness Dominic stood by her side and always pulled Waverly out of any confrontation, keeping her morality clause intact. Each time her hero kept her out of harm's way, it became harder for Waverly to concentrate on her goals. Every morning before working with Dominic, Waverly gave herself a little pep talk and reminded herself that she needed the crown, not a man. Dominic didn't make the resistance any easier showing up in a pair of jeans and a plain white T-shirt or even a suit on some occasions. Waverly's first thought after seeing him was to rip off his shirt and run her hands over every inch of his muscular body. Dominic's body wasn't just a turn-on. His mind and patience were, as well. He took the verbal jokes about being Mr. Southwood or Miss Southwood's handmaiden in stride. The memes died down a bit as she spent more time in Southwood. However, after the last event at a small county fair, someone took the infamous picture of Waverly tearfully handing over her tiara and made it appear she was exchanging her crown for a shovel.

Waverly enjoyed the local Southwood events she attended where she didn't have to share the spotlight with other beauty queens. Just before little kids went back to school, Waverly was able to emcee the annual bachelor auction, which every single—and not so single— woman loved to attend.

One of the better parts of being Miss Southwood and part of the Christmas Advisory Council was being able to spend extra time with Dominic. She enjoyed their camaraderie and she immensely enjoyed not having to talk about the pageant world all the time with him. He didn't pressure her about her family history or her relationship with her mother and she gathered early on he did not enjoy talking about his father. Thanks to sticking to her new diet, there were no more misdelivered pizzas, either. Dominic proved his muscle worth by helping her work out at the Southwood Premier Gym. He had a personal workout area at his ranch but Waverly didn't want to chance anything. It was hard enough watching his muscles flex or the gentle way his hands caressed her backside to help her with some of the workout machines.

People seemed to enjoy watching the two of them together. They were the beauty and the brawn. Together they traveled around town and made appearances at the Senior Citizen Center for donated vintage clothes for the Christmas parade for the participants to wear. During the week, Dominic worked in his garage. On the weekends she and Dominic—with Kenzie and Anson in tow—drove around and gathered donations from just about every decade possible from local sources.

Lexi offered to store the dresses in her boutique and alter them if needed. The list of Christmas parade participants grew each day. Waverly wondered if there'd be anyone standing on the sidelines to watch.

The biggest concern for Waverly right now was Lexi. Stephen Reyes had sent a group text to everyone; Lexi was in labor. Thankfully Waverly was with Dominic at the time in a 1970s Corvette, and he got Waverly to the hospital just in time to learn Lexi needed an emergency C-section. While they waited, Waverly couldn't help but wonder about her future. According to her life plan of obtaining tiaras, Waverly would be almost in her thirties before it was time to settle down and have children. A part of her heart ached at the idea of waiting so long.

Kimber, Lexi's niece, paced the floor. Stephen and his brother Nate had rearranged their lives to move to Southwood to take care of their nieces when their brother, Ken, and his wife passed away.

Waverly wrapped her arms around Kimber's shoulders to comfort her. Philly, her eight-year-old sister and a pageant queen in her own right, ran over to Waverly and Kimber to make herself a part of the group hug.

"She's going to be okay," said Amelia, Nate's wife. Amelia came into the picture last year; Waverly hadn't been in Southwood at the time, but she'd heard the stories. Amelia returned to Southwood hell-bent on revenge on Nate; she purchased Nate at the annual bachelor auction for the highest price to date. Waverly wondered whatever happened to the revenge plot. Clearly it backfired on her. The former reality show producer and now part owner of The Scoop, Southwood's premier ice-cream parlor, patted the girls on their backs. She knelt down to Philly's level. "She and the baby are in good hands. I vetted the doctors personally when I proposed a reality show in town."

"Yeah," Nate chimed in. "Everything is going to be fine."

Waverly gulped down a large lump in her throat. She prayed Stephen was right. She didn't know what she'd do if something happened to Lexi.

"Hey—" Dominic spoke up "—why don't I get everyone some coffee?"

Philly turned her head upward for approval from Amelia and Waverly. Nate answered for them, "No, you can't."

"How about some hot chocolate?" Dominic offered. "With marshmallows."

"Can I have as many as I want?" Philly asked.

Lips quivering at Dominic's gentleness, Waverly placed her hand over her heart. She'd been so busy all her life planning her pageants, she never stopped to think about a family. Waverly told herself she loved pageants. She did. But she wouldn't be in this world if it weren't for her mother. Yes, Jillian had sacrifices, but so had Waverly. She didn't have a traditional upbringing and missed out on a lot of typical teenage things, like sleepovers with friends. At a young age, Waverly had decided if she ever had children she would never force the pageant world on them. This tender side of Dominic's, however, made Waverly rethink her whole life, especially when he knelt to Philly's level.

"You may have two," Nate warned, putting two fingers in the air.

Dominic gave Philly a wink, which wiped away any worry lines off Philly's face. He held out his large hand for her to take. "Why don't you come with me and we'll get everyone something?"

Philly eagerly left the huddle to go off with Dominic. She squealed in delight when he picked her up to ride his shoulders. They left the waiting room and Waverly led Kimber over to the couch.

"Quite the man you have there," Amelia pointed out, bumping Waverly's shoulder when she sat down next to her.

"He's not my man," Waverly said, but she beamed. She loved the idea of Dominic being hers—more than she wanted to admit.

"Good to know."

The three ladies left in the waiting room all glanced up at the doorway. Waverly's lip moved upward at the sight of Vera. The current Miss South Georgia wore a white-and-royal-blue sash over a silver-and-royal-blue pageant gown. While Waverly wore her tiara, she paired it with something more casual, like her pink sweats— typical Saturday-afternoon attire for cleaning out the back of Grits and Glam Gowns.

"Hi, Vera." Amelia stood up and greeted the competition with her arms stretched out. "What are you doing here?"

Vera gave Amelia an air kiss on both cheeks and a light pat on the shoulders. "I was fulfilling my duties as Miss South Georgia, visiting the children, when I passed Philly in the corridor. She said Lexi was in labor. How is she?"

"She's fine," Kimber said coolly. "You should really go. This is for family."

Stiffening, Vera rolled her eyes. "I've known Lexi longer than any of you. If anyone deserves to be here, it's me."

"Everything okay, babe?"

Waverly leaned back in her seat at the sound of the familiar voice. The journalist who agitated her in the infamous interview sidled up to Vera's side. A camera hung around his neck with a guitar strap. His beady eyes bore down on Waverly, then widened with surprise.

"You've got to be kidding me." Waverly came to her feet and Kimber followed. "Get this jerk out of here."

"Jerk?" Vera's head bobbled back and forth. "This is Blu Fontaine."

"I don't care who the hell he is," Waverly snapped. "You know exactly what he did."

"Is this the jerk who antagonized you?" Kimber asked, her hands on her hips.

"Yes, it is." Waverly fought the urge to clutch the opening of her shirt. This was the same man who asked her to take her top off and tried to lure her into his bed.

"Now, hold on a minute." Blu held his hands out to slow everyone down. "I believe we have a misunderstanding."

"The only misunderstanding is you thinking that tiara meant you could hit on me and then manipulate the footage to make me look crazy."

"What?" Vera reared her head back.

"Babe," he sputtered.

"You weren't supposed to hit on her."

Hearing the truth come out, Waverly's blood boiled. Anger washed over her. Vera always played dirty behind closed curtains. She was known to take someone's heels, hide a bow from a violinist moments before talent portions and even tattle to the pageant committee when contestants got together to party. But this took the cake. She was evil. "I knew you had something to do with it."

She balled her fists. In her lifetime Waverly had never struck a person, but she'd be damned if Vera hadn't brought her the brink of violence. Waverly advanced a step. Vera didn't back down. Instead the other woman squared her shoulders and tilted her chin forward, daring her.

"Go ahead." Vera sneered. "You'll be just like Johnny Del Vecchio."

The mere mention of Waverly's ex sent rage all through her being. The first time Waverly met the Morality Committee had been when they'd showed up at a street race Johnny was in. The commotion brought the local reporters, who were champing at the bit to expose unruly beauty queens. The committee had been sent an anonymous tip. Waverly had always suspected Vera. "Another thing you had something to do with."

"You can't prove a thing," Vera said, miffed.

"I got enough." Waverly seethed, raising a fist.

"Whoa!" someone yelled into the waiting room.

Several people stopped the interaction. The room spun as someone grabbed Waverly around the waist and twirled her to the other side of the waiting room. Anson tugged Vera out of the way; Blu stood behind his camera, taking pictures, and in the entrance of the delivery room stood Stephen, dressed in mint-green scrubs and a face mask. Waverly didn't need to see his entire face to read the look of horror in his eyes. Everyone stopped yelling and moving. Someone set Waverly right on her feet.

"I hate to interrupt," Stephen said, "but it's a boy. Lexi and Kenneth are resting but doing fine. Not like I can say the same for everyone out here."

"Ladies," Mayor Ascot said to the room of witnesses from the waiting room, the police chief and members of the Morality Committee, a group of former beauty queens committed to preserving the sanctity of the tiaras and titles of regional pageants. "We can't have altercations going on in our city. The emergency Morality Committee has come to order."

What a waste of time, Dominic thought to himself. His foot twitched as he waited for the chance to speak with Waverly. Back at the hospital, he knew they'd shared more than just a moment together, where he realized they were on the same page in life. He wanted a family. Given his history, or lack thereof, with his deadbeat father, Dominic had never wanted children until today. First he needed to get her out of this stupid witch hunt.

If Dominic hadn't seen this with his own eyes, he wouldn't have believed such a thing existed. The reporter he met on the docks at the Magnolia Palace sat in the front row, jotting down notes. Dominic hated the helpless feeling of watching Waverly in a chair on the stage of the conference room in city hall. He folded his arms across his chest to keep from crashing the stage and choking the mayor. There'd been no physical altercation. Dominic had seen it himself when he walked back into the waiting room with beverages for everyone. Someone did, however, film the confrontation and send it to the local news. The video showed more of a scuffle than anything else, but someone in the span of twelve hours already managed to turn a few photos of Waverly into a meme, superimposing her face on a bull and Vera's onto a matador and shading her in red. Someone went even as far as placing a red tiara in Vera's hands.

"I wasn't doing anything," Vera said, pressing her hand to her chest. "She attacked me."

"If she attacked you," Kimber spit out toward the stage, "you wouldn't be here."

"See what I'm dealing with?" Vera whined.

Dominic probably would have seethed as well, but his cell phone buzzed in his pocket. Since he recognized the area code, he swiped the red icon to end the call. He needed to focus on Waverly. He knew how important getting into the Miss Georgia Pageant was to her. This scuffle might cost her the second chance she'd been given, and despite his growing feelings for her, wouldn't want to risk her dream.

"Vera, please," Mayor Ascot said. "You both have signed a morality clause for your designated pageants and you both are skating on thin ice. I've got reporters from all three surrounding cities hounding me concerning this bickering the two of you have been doing at the joint fairs and events."

Waverly sat onstage with her hands folded in her lap, knees together. A smile was frozen on her face. Dominic couldn't tell what was going on in her mind and it killed him. His phone buzzed again, and again Dominic declined the call.

Three ladies sat in front of the stage at a long table. The woman who did the most talking wore a pair of cat-eye black-rimmed glasses on top of her pinched nose. She read from a pink-and-silver clipboard and pushed her glasses up on her nose once she looked up.

"Ladies," she said, "I can't express how disappointed I was to hear of this unfortunate interaction between you two. Miss Vera, you were at the hospital for a visit to the children's wing. What if the parents or, worse, the children, saw you two?"

"Miss Lexi Pendergrass Reyes was in labor," Vera said as if that explained it all.

It must have. The three committee members nodded their heads in unison.

"If I may," Mayor Ascot said, speaking up, "it is my understanding both women are vying for a spot in the Miss Georgia Pageant."

"Prior to this altercation," said the spokesperson, "they were. As of today we don't know what to do. Neither of you ladies act like you want the title."

Waverly raised her hand while Vera scoffed.

"Mrs. Ramsey," Waverly began. "Vera and I have

pageanted all our lives. This is all we know. We were both emotionally charged at the hospital. Our coach was in labor and underwent an emergency Cesarean. To say our stress levels were at the highest is an understatement." Waverly rose from her seat and walked toward the edge of the stage. "While our actions were not mature or a representation of the Pageant Morality Committee, I beg of you all to take into consideration that this lone incident dealt with Lexi, and it will never happen again."

The thought to start a slow clap crossed Dominic's mind. If she didn't have the voice of an angel to woo judges, she needed to get into acting or at least do a monologue for the next portion of her pageant. His phone buzzed again but Dominic focused on his beauty queen onstage.

"We understand the emotional stress between the two of you," Mrs. Ramsey began, "but we cannot allow these shenanigans to continue, especially by contestants participating in the Miss Georgia Pageant. We arrived today in Southwood with a simple solution. We cannot have you or the other contestants in the region in the next-level pageant."

The crowd, Dominic included, booed.

Mrs. Ramsey turned to everyone and shushed them with a finger pressed to her lips, then turned back to the ladies onstage. "With all of the local entries for Miss Georgia, we have decided there are too many girls to put forward. Therefore we recommend a runoff before the Miss Georgia application. Whoever wins this region will get the full support of the Morality Committee." Before the booing began again, Mrs. Ramsey hammered her gavel on her table. She and her committee left the conference room swiftly.

While Vera rushed off the stage in tears, Waverly stood in her spot, frozen. Dominic's insides ached at the sight of her. She looked lost. The crown meant that much to her. Waverly's group from the hospital bombarded the stage and patted her back. He waited patiently for his opportunity to approach her. Once again his cell phone buzzed. This time Dominic answered.

"This better be good," he growled.

"Dominic Crowne?"

"This is him." Dominic pulled the phone away from his ear and double-checked the number. "Who is this?"

"Mr. Crowne, this is Dr. Brock Rayland, a neurologist at Phoenix General. I'm here with your father."

Confused, Dominic shook his head at the phone. "Why are you calling me?"

"Because your father is dying of chronic traumatic encephalopathy, and he listed you as his next of kin."

After the embarrassing showdown in the waiting room at the hospital and the humiliating results of the hearing, Waverly didn't blame Dominic for needing a break from whatever it was they were working on. Last month seemed so long ago. After learning about the absurd runoff, the first person Waverly needed to speak with was Dominic. She needed to apologize for the drama she'd dragged him and his shop into.

The radio silence killed her in the beginning. Was he fed up with her and the pageant world? Waverly wanted to give Dominic the benefit of the doubt, that he didn't abandon her. Waverly tried to reason with logic. Maybe he had to go out of the country. He did mention his friends overseas. At least he could have given her a call or sent a note or something, right? She'd thought they were friends. A friendship shouldn't ache as much as it did. Waverly even did the proverbial drive-by at his ranch with her coworkers. Andrew Mason, who ran Grits and Glam Gowns as well as Lexi's pageant-focused Grits and Glam Studios, located on the first floor of the building next door, took Waverly out for a ride one night. Fall leaves gathered around the piled-up newspapers, and cars lined the driveway, but there was no sign of life. Waverly pathetically traveled down to Alisha's apartment on the pretense of borrowing a cup of sugar, and even she had left. Her neighbors said they hadn't seen Alisha or her pet pig in weeks.

Waverly's French-manicured fingers hovered over the one photograph she had of her and Dominic together, taken moments after she'd won the crown. She frowned and pushed herself away from the cash register at Grits and Glam Gowns. She'd spent this morning listening to the band at Southwood Middle School prepare for the upcoming Christmas recital and it was painful to listen to. The tap-dancing session next door in the studios didn't help the headache threatening behind Waverly's temples.

"Girl, you look beat," said Chantal, coming through the kitchen. Waverly adored Chantal Hairston, who gave up a financial career with her father's firm in Orlando to follow her dreams of teaching dance. "Why don't you get some fresh air, stretch your legs…or eat a cupcake? The Cupcakery is kicking off their fall pumpkin menu early this year."

Waverly glanced down at her hips and shook her head no. "Maybe after the runoff."

Chantal frowned and turned up her nose. "So silly," she mumbled with a shake of her head. It was easy for Chantal to eat whatever she wanted; the woman danced every day. "I'm serious about getting some fresh air. Go for a walk and bring me back a cupcake. I'll hold things down."

Not wanting to argue, Waverly slipped her heels back on her feet and headed out the doors onto Sunshine Street and turned the corner onto the Grits and Glam Studios side of the street. Through the windows, Waverly smiled and waved at the group of preschool girls standing in two lines, practicing their tap-dancing routines. Despite the bright sun, a chill whipped through the air. Waverly tugged the long sleeves of her thin, dark blue T-shirt. She took the tiara off for a brief moment to loosen her hair from the bun on top of her head. Her tresses warmed the back of her neck. With school still in session, the streets were quiet except for the faint sound of the band practicing in the distance. The sweet smell of apples floated down the street from The Cupcakery. Waverly hadn't stepped foot in the bakery since the announcement of the runoff. She figured she'd follow the fragrance coming from the oven. Passing in front of Crowne's Garage would be a sheer coincidence, right?

"Care for a cup of coffee?"

The deep voice startled her. Waverly spun around in her heels and found Anson coming out of the old post office building. "Anson," Waverly breathed as she clutched her heart. Anson closed the doors to the old gray building with a set of large brass skeleton keys. He shoved the key ring into the pocket of his black pea-coat. The weather was breezy but not that bad. "This building has been closed since I got here. I didn't expect anyone to come outside."

"Sorry." He half smiled. "I didn't mean to scare you. And this building won't be empty for long. I've got the City Council to agree to sell it." Anson nodded his head across the street toward the business next door to Grits and Glam Gowns. "I've even got Reyes Realty in the works."

Lexi's husband owned the space next door to her business. Stephen Reyes was the number one real estate agent in town. "Cool," Waverly managed to say.

"And with any luck, we'll get rid of this eyesore on the corner," Anson said, pointing toward the corner of Sunshine Boulevard and Sunshine Street. Grits and Glam Studios faced an entrance of Crowne's Garage. A lump formed in Waverly's throat. Clueless, Anson continued, "Crowne left town, left his workers and even left a stack of bills. Bastard put a few people out of work because of his disappearing act."

"No one's heard from him?" Waverly asked, trying not to sound too eager. The two of them fell into step. In the weeks since the hospital incident, Anson had paid special attention to Waverly. Why she was so startled when he came out of the building baffled her. Anson managed to pop up wherever Waverly went these days. She expected to see him at the local events and the Christmas Advisory Council, but he also turned up and offered to walk her home on the nights she worked at Grits and Glam Studios.

Anson shook his head. "It seemed like the two of you were friends," he said, then bumped his shoulder against hers, "or at least, I thought you two were just friends."

"We are, or were," said Waverly.

"Not as close as you thought, huh?"

She didn't know how to answer. What was she supposed to say? "Well, who knows?"

"No one knows," answered Anson. "Which is why going on with shutting this place down is for the better. We don't want Southwood to turn into a ghost town."

Shutting down seemed so official and final. Waverly shook her head and kept walking, crossing over to Main Street toward The Cupcakery. Just because she couldn't indulge didn't mean Chantal couldn't. Anson still followed.

"Waverly," he began. "I know you and Dominic worked out some deal where he drove you around to pick up the clothing Kenzie Swayne requested, but I want you to know I'm here for you if you need someone to drive you around. I know he's disappeared on you."

"I appreciate that," Waverly mumbled. She hated to think of having to rely on Anson. His favors came with an unspoken price tag. "I don't want to count Dominic out too soon."

"You don't owe him a thing." Anson seethed. "What has he done for you?"

Taken aback by the mayor's bluntness, Waverly stopped walking. "I at least owe him the benefit of doubt, Mr. Mayor. Without Dominic's help, I wouldn't have this crown." She pointed to the top of her head, where the Miss Southwood tiara she had to wear whenever she was in public caught the sunlight and flickered off the glass window of The Scoop.

Anson shrugged his broad shoulders. "I get that you represented Crowne's Garage for Miss Southwood. You garnered more business for him while he was here. But that's all the man wanted from you. Unlike me. I couldn't care if you went on to be Miss Georgia or anything else. Your best role would be by my side as Mrs. Wilson. We're destined to be together."

Not appreciating the dismissal of her hard work as a beauty queen, Waverly rolled her eyes and tried to remember her manners. "We've had this conversation before, when I first arrived in Southwood. You know I am not interested in settling down with anyone," Waverly clarified in a clipped tone. She averted her eyes back toward the garage.

"I hope you're not waiting on him," Anson sneered.

Waverly shook her head, hating the uncomfortable turn of this conversation. "I have my goals."

"Good, because I hate to be the one to break it to you, Waverly, but you were nothing more than a project for Mr. Crowne. Like his cars, he put you back together, and now you're off for the next big thing. Which brings you to me. His job is done and now I'm here to help."

Waverly wanted to dispute Anson and put him in his place. Every fiber of her being told her Anson was wrong, but as the official fall season kicked in and holidays slipped from Halloween to Thanksgiving, Waverly accepted the hard truth: Dominic was gone.

Chapter 6

Over the weeks since she'd accepted Dominic's departure, Waverly concentrated on her runoff. She told herself she was no longer torn by glimpses of the traditional life outside the pageant. With the runoff coming, Waverly was ready to secure the support of the committee and be nominated to go forward to participate in Miss Georgia. The floor-to-ceiling window offered the perfect view of the evening hustle and bustle of the townspeople of Southwood, Georgia. Christmas garlands outlined the doors of the local businesses, accompanied by a big red bow above the doors. Red, white and green lights hung from building to building, crisscrossing the streets. The view offered an inside look of what some families were getting for dinner tonight—Chinese takeout from across the street or pizza from the parlor adjacent to Grits and Glam Studios. Cars heading to their suburban homes crowded the cobble-stone streets, along with people getting ready to head home or who came to town for some of Southwood's fine restaurants, like Sonya's, right around the corner, or Valencia, which Waverly had helped open with a giant pair of scissors four months ago.

Waverly knew who was heading on dates and who was getting some early Christmas shopping done. But most of all, for Waverly the view offered the biggest piece of gossip for the night. The doors to Crowne's Garage were finally reopening.

Dominic had returned.

Whether she said his name out loud or in her head, Dominic's frame was conjured up and appeared at the rolling garage door to his shop. Even with the sunset shadowing his face, Waverly knew his body. A low, guttural sound rippled in the back of her throat at the sight of his wide, muscular shoulders and tapered waist. His large arms lingered over the handle above his head, causing his biceps to bulge. The fitted jeans he wore hung a perfect inch or two just below his hips and hugged those massive tree trunk legs.

Waverly controlled her pulse beating against her wrists by pulling her hands into her lap. How could he cause this much nervousness after three months with no word? She ought to march right over there and thank him for leaving. This had allowed Waverly to shine at pageant appearances without the threat of gossip. She delved into not just the pageant but making new friends in town. She had a life. Turning her face from the window, Waverly rested her right hand on the arm of the hot-pink sofa to block out Dominic and focused on the two little girls standing in the center of the stage used for the talent portions of pageant shows. Old glitter twinkled under the fluorescent lights on the floor beneath the twins' pink patent leather Mary Jane shoes. Black scuff marks were scratched into the black topping of the stage from the tap dance show-down yesterday for tryouts for the Christmas pageant. Little handprints smudged the mirrored walls along the ballet barre. Larger handprints also smudged the glass at a higher point. Chantal taught beginner ballet to some of the ladies in town.

Maybe we need to get new flooring, Waverly thought as Novella and Keisha Irby hit the high note at different times. Waverly winced from the noise, and the back of her neck ached when she tried to crane her head toward the window. This time of year, the sun set earlier than usual. The figure at the garage, however, remained.

"No. Oh my God," cried the girls' mother, Rhonda, from the other end of the hot-pink couch. Rhonda turned out to be the lady from the initial Christmas Advisory Council meeting in all leopard print. When the news of the squabble spread around town, Rhonda approached Waverly and let her know she was all right in her book. Rhonda now set down boxed Advent calendars Waverly had put together for the parents of pageant girls, and pressed her gold nails against her temples. A dozen gold bangles around her wrists jingled.

The girls stopped their singing and twitched nervously onstage in their matching pink-and-white polka-dot leggings and lightweight pink sweaters. "Tell me you hear this new high-pitched dolphin sound they're doing, Waverly."

Thankful for the distraction, Waverly turned away from the window—again. She needed to process the thin, strange twinge in her heart. This man turned his back on her, abandoned her without a word. What did it matter if Dominic returned to Southwood?

"Maybe we need to take a break?" Waverly offered, standing up. Her coral-colored toes wiggled in her brown leather gladiator sandals as she headed toward the break room. Lexi always kept snacks and drinks in the fridge to rehydrate herself after a jog around town while getting her back to her prebaby body. Waverly wished she'd look as good as Lexi had the day after giving birth. "We've been going at this for a half hour straight."

This was her last appointment for the evening at Grits and Glam Studios. Waverly loved working with the local children, molding them into the perfect presenters onstage for pageants or whatever the need. Lately, with the Christmas holidays rapidly approaching, she'd donned her vocal coach hat when she wasn't campaigning for votes for the runoff.

As if on cue, Andrew poked his blond head in from the kitchen. His cheeks were rosy and blue eyes sparkled with mischief. "Did someone say a break?"

"You know what?" Rhonda asked, standing up and smoothing down her red dress with gold accents. "We should probably head on over to church." Her announcement evoked a whine from her girls. "I can't see wasting your time anymore, Waverly."

"Don't leave," pleaded Andrew. Waverly cocked a brow at him. "Waverly's just received a special delivery, and I can't imagine her keeping these to herself." He stepped back into the kitchen. As the reigning Miss Southwood, Waverly often received bouquets of flowers or signature dishes from any event she attended. The flowers always went back to the newly opened South-wood Elderly Care Community Center. The food, Waverly often shared.

"I'm sorry for the interruption." Waverly offered a smile of apology toward Miss Rhonda, the formal name she called her when they were in the studio. On the rare occasions Waverly hung out at happy hour, Miss Rhonda became Randy Rhonda on account of how crazy things got when her twins were with their father for the weekend. "I'm not expecting anything."

"Don't be sorry," said Rhonda, patting Waverly on the back. "When other people get surprises, I feel like I've received one, as well. And this will give me something to report back at prayer services."

Waverly gave Rhonda the eye—the one she learned from her mother, Jillian Leverve. Rhonda, also being a mom, recognized the eye and held her hands up in surrender. "Okay, okay. I'm just going to get my prayer on. My lips are sealed." For emphasis or plain old show, Rhonda made a zip-and-lock motion with her hands against her lips.

Suddenly, the mouthwatering scent of sweet, decadent chocolate danced through the air. The twins squealed in delight, causing Waverly to spin at her piano bench. Her mouth nearly dropped to the floor at the oversize bouquet of cupcakes carried in by Andrew. The six-foot-plus assistant's entire upper body was concealed by the cupcake arrangement. Only his legs and hands were visible.

"Can we receive the surprise, too, Mama?" asked Novella.

"Please," Keisha chimed in, her brown hands folded under her chin as if in prayer.

"What on earth?" Waverly peered around the arrangement of cupcakes: chocolate with chocolate sprinkles or designs, French vanilla with fluffy flower drops, pink strawberry drizzled with chocolate and sliced strawberries. A trail of dark chocolate curls formed behind Andrew from his walk into the studio. A white gift card stuck out from a stem in the center of the peach cupcake and bore her first initial, W. Someone had clout. These cupcakes were made only during the summertime. It had been months since she'd had one.

"Someone knows you have a sweet tooth," Andrew cooed, winking at the twins. Waverly held the card close to her chest, knowing he wanted to know who sent her these. He scoffed at Waverly's attempt at privacy and focused on the twins. "Look, girls, these Pretty in Pearlicious Pink cupcakes match your dresses."

"Someone doesn't know I'm entering a runoff for the Miss Georgia Pageant." Waverly groaned. She pointed toward the girls, who squealed in anticipation of her next few words. Waverly raised another brow at Rhonda. "I can't eat these by myself. You guys will be doing me a favor if you take a few off my hands."

With a playful dramatic huff, Rhonda reluctantly nodded. "Fine, if we must. But if I can't fit into my Christmas dress, I'm blaming you," she said, grabbing a caramel-swirled cupcake and licking off the creamy frosting. "Come on, girls. Let's go."

Waverly waited for the bells above the door to stop jingling as the young family left to pull the card away from her chest. Andrew still leered, but he knew all her secrets anyway. A man who knew your true weight was your best friend.

"What's it say?" Andrew bounced in his red Crocs. "Who are they from?"

The strange feeling Waverly couldn't describe from a few moments ago came back as she read the letters on the card.

"Holy hell, Waverly." Andrew gasped. His shoes squeaked against the hardwood floors. "Mmm, Thanksgiving might be over but I certainly know who I'm thankful for. Did you see who reopened up shop across the street?"

No need to turn around. Waverly knew. "Yes."

"After three months of radio silence, Dominic Crowne is back in town?"

Not able to take it, Waverly turned around to face the window. Her shoulders brushed against the stargazed Andrew. The lamp in the garage flickered above his head. There was no mistaking Dominic's handsome face or his cockiness. He had the nerve to salute her before disappearing inside.

"Yep," Waverly said, "and he wants to see me at my earliest convenience."

"So do you think your little trick worked?"

Dominic turned toward the sound of his sister's voice. His eyes needed to adjust to the lights being turned back on inside Crowne's Garage. Alisha stood by the register and flipped through three months' worth of mail. By now Dominic's molars were in perpetual pain after grinding his teeth together to keep from saying something hurtful to Alisha. Thanks to her, Crowne's Garage had been abandoned for the last three months. Mayor Ascot took it upon himself to post vacancy signs on the doors. Dominic was sure the act was petty and malicious, but he had other things to worry about besides dealing with the cowardly man. When Dominic took off to Arizona, Alisha considered herself to be on vacation, as well. He should have had a clue when he booked her Thanksgiving flight out of Miami. Without telling his siblings, Dominic flew out to care for their estranged father. When the end came near, he called the rest of the family in time, and they buried John after finally getting years of hostility off their chests. Not much of a great Thanksgiving weekend. Dominic chartered a flight for him and Alisha to return to Southwood this morning. Their brothers, Darren and Dario, were coming back to Southwood for the holidays in a few weeks.

"Tiffani told me you paid her folks a lot of money for the cupcake arrangement you sent over," Alisha went on. "What did you write in the note?"

"I wrote in the note," he began, "for her to come over at her earliest convenience."

Dominic didn't expect to see Waverly anytime soon. She probably hated him for leaving her in the dark for three months. After the runoff announcement back in August, he had every intention to speak with her, but the call about his father's near-death experience took precedence. Dominic would have been damned before letting his father die without giving him a piece of his mind. He took off without a word, fully expecting to bury his father before September rolled around. Damn John Crowne and his penchant for hanging on to dear life and lingering just until Thanksgiving. Dominic had embarrassed himself by not getting in touch with Waverly.

Because of his visit to John's alleged deathbed in August, the man hung on to life for a few more months, causing Dominic to break his promise to Waverly. He'd promised to help her out in gaining her Miss Georgia crown. He hated having to go back on his word. He felt like a heel for doing so, especially with John being the reason. Dominic had seethed with burning anger when John did not die right away. Dominic had wanted to curse the man and return to Waverly. But the moment Dominic had stormed into John's hospital room and locked eyes with his father, something changed. John Crowne, barely sitting upright, began bawling and apologizing. He was embarrassed for anyone to find out he'd caved so easily. For the first time in his life, Dominic experienced forgiveness and in doing so, a Zen feeling had washed over him. He needed to stay for closure. By October, Dominic had decided on what was best for Waverly and her quest for her next tiara. He'd kept tabs on her winning over crowds at the Labor Day picnic held in the park, judging a Halloween contest for the kids at Four Points General Hospital and arriving on a float for the Veterans Day parade. Dominic even went as far as following the pageant world on social media. Waverly stood out from the other Southern pageant queens forced into the runoff. If everyone voted today, she would win hands down. Even the vicious memes of Waverly losing her Miss South Georgia crown died down and were replaced with other things going on in social media.

In order for Waverly to continue on her successful pageant path, Dominic wondered if it was best to stay away. Besides, Waverly probably hated him by now or at least wrote him off. Dominic didn't blame her. He'd dropped everything for a man who never gave his family a second thought. Dominic and Waverly had been on the way to something—what exactly, he wasn't sure, but they had a deep connection.

Alisha scoffed and tapped a political flyer for a local election on top of the credit card machine. "She's Miss Southwood. Tiffani says she's rarely in town, you know, doing all those beauty queen duties and campaigning to secure her spot for the Miss Georgia Pageant."

"I know exactly who she is," Dominic bit out, trying to remember Alisha's naïveté. She had no clue of the damage her vacation had done. He should have told her from the beginning about John's illness. Dominic had meant to protect his siblings by not telling them about John at first. He'd left a note at Crowne's Garage for Alisha that he'd had to leave town. Alisha had assumed Dominic went off on another business trip. "I'm the one who made sure she got the tiara."

"You bought her the dress and paid the entry fee under your bogus Miss Crowne's Garage title," Alisha said with a droll eye roll. "I'm pretty sure her beauty had a lot to do with it."

Ah yes. The thought of Waverly's pretty heart-shaped face made him smile, wiping away all the frustration. A few moments ago he'd been able to spy on her before the power kicked back on and exposed his position like some stalker. When he stepped outside to get some air, he'd spied her long legs, the same thing that had attracted him the first time they met. Tonight Waverly had been wearing a pair of sandals that wrapped around her calves and went up to her knees. One day soon he was going to find out how nice it was having her legs wrapped all the way around his waist.

"Hey." Alisha snapped her blue-painted nails in his face. "Earth to Dominic. Keep or throw away?"

Dominic focused on the flyer for the election they'd just missed. "Throw it away."

"What do you have here?" Dominic picked up one of the stacks Alisha sorted.

Hamilton the pig grunted at his feet, almost causing him to trip. "Move, pig."

"Don't be mean to him," Alisha said, poking out her bottom lip. "He's been through a lot."

A lot, meaning Hamilton had to fly out to Arizona with the rest of the animal cargo. Alisha didn't get an official letter claiming her need for emotional support. "Whatever, Alisha. I still can't believe you put him in a suit for Pop's funeral."

"You got mad at me for putting him in a tutu, so make up your mind."

"I'm trying to make up my mind as to whether or not I'm going to fire you," Dominic growled. Thank God he was able to make it to city hall this afternoon to get the lights to the business turned on, and that they'd honored his six-month advance payment by turning them on a few minutes ago.

"I didn't realize your bill wasn't automatically paid out of your account. You ought to keep a record of it."

"Like a bookkeeper?"

Alisha's light brown face lit up. "Yeah, exactly."

Pressure built against his temples when he gnashed his teeth. Dominic resisted pinching the bridge of his nose. Alisha had been through a lot already. Reminding her she'd screwed up his business wasn't going to help. Did she maliciously leave without making sure someone was in charge? No, Dominic answered himself.

"You started up Crowne's Garage out on your ranch a year ago," Alisha went on, defending herself. "I figured when you opened a garage in town, you were good with the banks and they just worked the light bill into your rent. How was I supposed to know?"

"Don't worry," Dominic said finally. "I'm sending you to school to learn."

Dominic ignored the protesting whine from his sister, aware she hated school. Funny, considering that school had saved him from a life of misery like his father. In the last few conversations Dominic had with his father, John explained his fear of not being good enough for his family since he did not have an education.

"I hate school," Alisha announced. "I'm not good at it like you."

"You'll learn to love it." Dominic pushed away from the register and stormed off into his office to change into a work jumper. He didn't have a lot of overalls in the shop—another thing messed up when he'd left Alisha in charge. She forgot his dry cleaning. Tomorrow he'd have to go to the cleaners and pick up his overdue items. Alisha was still sorting the mail when he came back through the garage. She rolled her eyes. Dominic expected the silent treatment for the next few days. No skin off his nose; Dominic welcomed the silence. He went back to work, stretching his six-foot-five-inch frame down on the rolling creeper.

And in his absence and with Alisha's mistakes, Dominic lost his mechanics and additional staff. Dominic reminded himself to take responsibility for the demise of Crowne's Garage. He never should have left Alisha in charge. Hell, it was a good thing he'd bought her condo flat out; otherwise she'd be out of a place and would have to move in with him at the ranch.

Dominic didn't realize he'd been so engrossed until

Alisha kicked the bottom of his work boot. "I know you can hear me."

"I'm working, Alisha."

As if to verify, Hamilton crawled underneath the old vehicle and sneezed, stirring up more dust and dirt. Dominic tried to move out of the way of the pig and ended up cutting a line, which leaked thick black liquid on the front of his coveralls.

"What are your plans with Waverly?" Alisha asked.

With a clamp, Dominic stopped the leak, but he'd still stained the material of his coveralls. Dominic maneuvered his shoulders to get out of the top portion. "What?"

"I need to be clear," said Alisha. "I mean, if I run into her, I need to know what to say."

"I don't need you to help," Dominic grunted. "I can manage all by myself to ask Waverly to help me look good in front of everyone." The sneeze he'd been holding in blasted out, causing Dominic to hit his head on the pipe above him.

"Bless you."

That did not sound like Alisha's voice.

Using his feet to help roll him out from underneath the car, Dominic found himself staring up at Waverly's equally shocked face.

The original bravado Waverly felt disappeared when Dominic rolled out on the wheeler and stood up. A hard lump formed in her throat, causing her to lose focus and her words. Had Dominic's muscles got bigger in his absence?

Dominic leaned against the hood of the car she'd seen Mr. Myers, the retired high school history teacher, drive around town on Sundays. A slow, cocky grin spread across his face. "You came."

From where she stood in his garage, braced against the back of a maroon Toyota, Waverly cocked her head to the side and admired the pair of coveralls he wore. The front was opened and pushed down, exposing the white T-shirt that stretched across the taut muscles of his chest and gripped those giant biceps of his. Waverly licked her lips and dragged her eyes from his body.

"I was curious about what you needed to say to me."

"I'm sorry," Dominic breathed.

Waverly shrugged. "For what? You didn't do anything."

"I abandoned you."

A lump formed in Waverly's throat. "You were embarrassed. I understand." She was ashamed of her actions. Dominic didn't want to be around a woman with so much drama.

"Embarrassed?" Dominic choked. "For what?"

"My behavior at the hospital."

"Your behavior?" He laughed. "You mean the way you went into full-on beast mode at that brat? You never looked sexier."

Feeling naked, Waverly folded her arms across her chest. "The words sound like a compliment but your tone is more insulting."

"Never insulting." Dominic's deep, calm voice sent a ripple of chills down Waverly's spine. "The city loves you. They voted you Miss Southwood."

Waverly waved off his flattery with the flick of her wrist. "I was voted in by a panel of judges, one of whom happened to be your fraternity brother."

"Are we going to stand here and argue over your popularity again?"

What she wanted was an answer about where he'd been but asking meant she cared. And Waverly told herself she no longer cared. Whatever Dominic considered popular in small Southwood did not compare to his when it came down to those billionaire associates of his. Okay, so fine, in his absence Waverly had thumbed through the last few issues of *Forbes*. Dominic rubbed elbows with royalty, folks who wore real diamonds in their tiaras, not Swarovski crystals.

"You may have confidence in me, and maybe even the town, but the Morality Committee doesn't." Waverly didn't have to be a psychic to know what his next word was going to be.

"F—"

She held her finger up in the air and shook her head. Waverly glanced around the nighttime scene of Southwood. No one was on the streets now. "Need I emphasize the morality part?"

"I am not the one heading for the Miss Georgia Pageant. Why do I have to watch my language?"

"My title puts me around children. I can't have anyone hanging around who is swearing like a sailor." Waverly pressed her back against the car behind her, the metal cooled her heated thighs. "I don't want to take any chances, Dominic, and lose my shot. I thought you understood. I have to win the runoff."

"You're a shoo-in. I've been following you on social media."

Waverly gulped at the idea of Dominic caring enough. "Did you need anything else from me?"

His eyes went toward the scoop neck of her teal T-shirt.

Waverly tugged at the hem to distract him from the swell of her breasts. Cool air rippled against her skin. Dominic cocked his head to the side and Waverly swore his eyes moved toward her hips.

With a huff, Waverly rolled her eyes. "I'm leaving."

Dominic took one long step toward her, catching her by the wrist. Her pulse quickened. "I'm sorry," he said softly. His thumb traced circles against her bones and veins. Waverly willed herself not to shiver. She avoided Dominic's penetrating stare, glancing outside at the Salvation Army Santa ringing his silver bell. "But you did ask the question."

"Seriously Dominic," said Waverly. She didn't move her hand and had no idea why she let him hang on to her except she liked the feel of him.

"I am trying to plan something nice."

"Aren't you a regular Kris Kringle?" Waverly said, her voice dripping with snark. "You just come to town doing favors for people?"

The fluorescent lights caught the few highlights of his hair. "I let the Christmas Advisory Council down. I want to make it up to them and I need your help."

"Offer them a free oil change."

"I have a lot more to offer than my grease monkey skills. I thought you knew that, Waverly."

Waverly gave his attire a raised brow. "How am I supposed to know? It's been a long time."

"Really, Waverly? It's been so long you've forgotten?"

"What I remember is your bright idea for me to enter Miss Southwood, against probably my only friend in town, and then you left." Waverly went back to folding her arms across her chest.

"There was more between us. I think you know that. I don't give a damn what your committee says or those stupid memes."

A pang seized her heart. She didn't want to discuss her humiliation. She realized now that trying to ask Dominic where he was made her fear his answer. He was embarrassed by her. Waverly didn't think she'd live down her past. Someone with a lot of time on their hands spliced the early-summer footage of Waverly taking her tiara off her head from her resignation with the fall video of her charging Vera at the hospital and made it appear as if Waverly tackled herself. With Christmas around the corner, someone also thought it would be funny to superimpose Waverly's face on a child's body; she was sitting on Santa's lap. Santa was asking what she wanted for Christmas and the imagination bubble drawn over Waverly's head showed her dreaming of tiaras.

"Your memes will die down, Waverly."

"Everything lasts forever on the internet," Waverly huffed.

A spell of silence fell between them. The lights hummed. A cool draft crept through the opened garage door. At this hour, most cars were already home, parked in their driveways. The businesses across the street were closing, all except the ice-cream parlor and the pizza shop. Common sense told her she ought to leave.

"So, back to your business?" Waverly turned her attention to Dominic again. Dominic stepped close to Waverly. "I am here now."

"And now you want the Christmas Council to forgive you?"

"I don't give a damn if they forgive me or not," Dominic barked. "I do care if you forgive me."

It would behoove her to step backward but Waverly refused to show her fear...or desire. Dominic smelled wonderful, spicy yet sweet at the same time. Waverly cocked a questioning brow at him.

"I never *left you*," Dominic clarified. His lips twitched for a moment before his eyes searched hers. "I couldn't be here for a while, but I am now."

Waverly licked her lips and squared her shoulders as he said, "I can't get confirmation on speaking during the council meeting. I'm guessing Mayor Ascot is pissed at me and has been talking crap about me in my absence. If you stand by me during the council meeting, they'll be more likely to say yes to my proposal."

"And the proposal is?"

"The Christmas parade is coming. I've got several cars stemming from the twenties to the present, and I am going to take care of drivers for the floats so folks won't miss any part of the parade."

"You're chauffeuring the parade to get everyone to like you? Or are you so hard up for customers?"

Dominic shook his head. His large hand reached out and brushed a lock of hair off her shoulder. "Haven't you heard by now? My company has turned record-breaking profits six years in a row."

"No."

"What a shame," he said, still with his hand on her shoulder. "I'm not here to increase my wealth. I am trying to fit in with the community. I'm trying to make things up with you."

Dominic rubbed the back of his head. The sleeves of his shirt rolled up on his biceps, revealing the decorative tattoos. Waverly inhaled deeply, not realizing she'd missed seeing them these last few months. She tried to remind herself that she was approaching her thirties now and was too old for crushes on the bad boys.

Waverly moved closer to the opening of the garage and prayed for the winter weather to settle in. The heat radiating from her body made her dizzy. She swore her attraction to bad boys came from the first time she was suspended from a pageant. Bad boys did this to her and Dominic was the ultimate.

Waverly felt her brow furrow. "Dominic, I can't give you what you want."

Dominic's hands went up in the air. "Do you think every man you come across wants you in his bed?"

Instead of answering, Waverly bit her bottom lip and pondered his question. If she answered honestly, she'd be considered conceited. Then again, she was already labeled that, thanks to the bastard, Blu. No matter what Blu said to her, Waverly was supposed to keep her composure and remain professional. She did neither. "Are you saying you want *nothing* sexual from me?"

Dominic licked his lips and cocked his head to the side again, this time making it apparent he was checking out her behind. "Don't ask me to lie, Waverly."

"Seriously?" Waverly placed her hands on her hips.

"Waverly, we didn't meet in a boardroom. We met at a bakery and we blatantly flirted with each other. We even kissed on our first date before your morality clause came into question." Dominic walked toward her, slow and deliberate steps.

"And then you helped with a pageant and then you disappeared."

"C'mon." Dominic groaned. "You're killing me here."

"Whatever, and that wasn't a date." Waverly backed up this time, ignoring her rapid heartbeat. "You shut out everyone in Southwood, including me." She stood with one foot inside the garage and the other outside. Dominic stopped right in front of her. He placed one hand above her head. The space next to his ear twitched as his jaw moved. Her heart skipped a beat.

"You're mad because you thought I left without saying goodbye?"

"I'm irritated. I thought we were at least friends." To create space between them, Waverly folded her arms. Her elbows pressed against his hard chest and still the friction fueled her desire. Dominic's disappearance had helped Waverly remain focused on earning her tiara back. "It's cool—while you were gone, I was able to get a lot of things done without any distraction."

"This kind of distraction?" Dominic dipped his head low and brushed his lips against hers.

It wasn't like Waverly had never been kissed. Or kissed by Dominic. If she thought the first time their lips touched her insides were set on fire, this one melted her system. Waverly dropped her hands to her sides. Hypnotized, she leaned into him, urging him to pursue her further. Dominic obliged. Their lips parted and tongues introduced themselves with a seductive, moan-evoking dance. Waverly pressed her hands against his chest. The beat of his heart pounded and echoed against her palms. Dominic's free hand scooped up Waverly's rear. He drew her against his hard body and even harder erection. Desire pumped through her veins. In the distance, laughter from a group of kids leaving from the park interrupted anything further. She hadn't realized she'd been lifted off her feet until Dominic set her back down on her sandals and her inner thigh scraped against his work jumpsuit from where she'd cocked her leg around his waist. *When? How? Geez.*

"Something like that?" Dominic asked.

Chapter 7

Without getting a final answer from Waverly last night, Dominic sat at the Christmas Advisory Council meeting Tuesday evening, wearing a blue suit his sister picked out for him. On second thought, it was more like her pet pig had picked out the suit when Alisha and Hamilton drove out to his ranch this morning. Hamilton oinked and snorted at the suit Alisha chose, which apparently met the pig's approval.

Alisha offered to come to the town meeting with him, but Dominic was almost thirty-one and did not need his younger sister to accompany him. He made his bed and he was going to have to face the music. Hopefully it'd be holiday music.

"Mr. Crowne."

Dominic looked up from the business plan in a leather folder in front of him. A sweet-faced older woman with crinkles and wrinkles at the corners of her dark eyes spoke his name with a smile.

"Miss Annie." Dominic greeted the woman as he rose from his seat. He extended his hand but she leaned in for a hug, wrapping his arms under his suit jacket. The top of her bluish hair reeked of hair spray, the same kind he imagined his grandmother used to use—the burn-a-hole-in-the-ozone kind.

"Welcome back, Mr. Crowne."

"Please, call me Dominic."

"I'm so glad you returned to town," said Miss Annie. "My grandson is going to return since you've reopened your garage. I wasn't sure he'd amount to much, but you inspired him to return to school for his engineering degree. Thank God he won't have to spend the rest of his life with grease under his nails."

Dominic grinned beyond his cringe. He'd hired her grandson, Billy, as a mechanic—a damn fine one, but still someone who grabbled under the hood and came home nightly with dirty nails.

"Billy's a hard worker. I'm glad to have him. And I apologize for any work Billy missed in my absence."

"Are you on the agenda for today?" Miss Annie asked. "I don't recall seeing your name."

"I believe there was a change sent out via email yesterday morning." Dominic went to find the green sheet handed to him at the entrance. He pulled it from underneath the minutes from last month's meeting. In his absence, Dominic had kept up with the agenda from the biweekly meetings.

Miss Annie scoffed and waved her hand. "I don't check that whole email thing. My grandson's tried to teach me but I'll never learn." She clasped her hands over Dominic's. "It's so good seeing you here. I can't wait to hear whatever you have to say."

"Hopefully everyone else will." Dominic patted her hand and flashed a smile. She said a few more flattering words and squeezed his biceps once more before joining her group of friends.

Dominic sat back down and opened his folder. His financial advisor thought he was crazy, but having one of his frat brothers managing your money helped. Craig Cozier, a financial wizard, knew what drove Dominic's Christmas spirit. Taking care of John and his estate gave Dominic an insight into living with the Ghosts of Christmas Past and Future. Dominic never wanted to be like his father, even more so now. John had gone to the grave with few to no friends and no family. Alisha and the twins had come but they had no interest in mending their relationships. The only woman he claimed he ever loved, Dominic's mother, hadn't bothered coming to the funeral. Dominic and his siblings didn't blame her. John never remarried and only lived to collect old-fashioned automobiles that sat in his field, collecting dust. Dominic's life wasn't too different from his father's. It was time for a change.

"Waverly," someone said in the room.

All eyes turned toward the holiday-decorated doors of the council room. People clapped at her presence and crowded around the beauty queen. A bare white pine Christmas tree stood next to a six-foot table filled with a cornucopia and fall-colored pinecones from last week's Thanksgiving meal. The best feature in the room, however, took Dominic's breath away.

Waverly Leverve stood straight and tall in a gray skirt, which stopped at her knees, and a tight-fitting, deep red short-sleeved sweater and a pair of matching heels. A tiara was perched on her brown tresses. Dominic's heart stopped. In the Ghost of Christmas Future's visit, he'd pictured Waverly in her condo, crying herself to sleep, and it had been his fault. He'd helped her earn the crown on top of her head now and then disappeared from her life. He promised himself he would never let that happen again. Insight into John's life had taught him well.

Like a graceful gazelle, Waverly glided across the dark gray carpet of the room. She stopped at each long table filled with Christmas committee members. Occasionally she'd flip her hair off her shoulders to laugh lightly at what someone said. Dominic admired the way she was attentive to everyone in the room. He'd never possessed the ability. Dominic liked being told what people needed and being left alone to the task at hand. This was not going to be the case here in Southwood. He needed to incorporate himself into the town. If he'd learned anything from his father's death, it was not to die alone.

"Hi," Waverly said, finally coming toward his table.

Dominic shifted in his seat in anticipation of finally having her to himself. He rose to his feet, not sure how to greet her. Last night they'd kissed. *If you wanted to call it a kiss*, he thought. It was more of a telling promise of how great they could be together. Hell, watching Waverly disappear through the front door of her condo was torture. As soon as she disappeared, he shut down the garage and took a cold shower in the back locker room.

Waverly extended her hand toward him for a shake. Automatically she also leaned in to kiss his cheek. How inappropriate it would be to greet her the way he wanted…by throwing everything off the table and kissing away all her lipstick.

"Waverly." Dominic swallowed down the excitement. What was he? Fourteen again? "Does your presence here mean you've agreed to help me out?"

"Hey, are you aware you're not on the agenda, Dominic?" Waverly said in a hushed voice. Her tortoiseshell-colored eyes darted around the room.

"I submitted a request to Mayor Ascot last night." Dominic reached in his pocket for his phone. He swiped the front and pulled up his email. No one had responded, but he did receive notification his message had gone through. "Are you going to answer my question?"

Waverly chuckled lightly and shifted her belongings. Dominic took her briefs off her hands and set them on the table. "You need to stop calling him that."

"Maybe."

"After careful consideration," Waverly said, "I've come to the conclusion your idea is sweet. Sure, I'll do whatever you want."

As a man, he was turned on by the words. He must have made a face or raised his brows because Waverly flattened her pouty lips and shook her head. "Behave yourself."

Dominic held his hand in the air and spread his fingers. "Scout's honor."

"I believe that's the sign for a science fiction show."

Dominic dropped his hands to pull out a chair for her. "Please, sit."

Allowing him to seat her, Waverly tucked a stray hair behind her ear and opened the top folder she'd brought in. "It's a good thing I am here."

"Tell me about it," Dominic mumbled. He took a seat

beside her, inhaling the crisp apple scent from her hair. Somehow the image of the two of them sitting on a red-and-white-checkered picnic blanket filled his mind.

"I have a five-minute spot I can share with you."

"Five?" Dominic asked. "What are you presenting to the council?"

"I'm reminding everyone about the Advent calendars I'm doing for the girls at Grits and Glam Studios. When I realized Southwood has so many wonderful shops, I thought calendars with coupons for free pageant lessons would be a great way to drum up business. The talent team is always seeking new blood for toddler pageants."

"I understand you started working on the talent team." Dominic didn't mean to sound surprised. He was rather glad. Waverly had the voice of an angel.

"As a favor to Lexi, while she's home taking care of the baby, and then once I win the runoff I'm going to stop so I can concentrate on training."

A gut punch hit Dominic. Had he stuck around in the waiting room, things between Waverly and Vera would never have escalated. Dominic had no doubt in his mind Waverly would win the runoff. This just secured the amount of time they'd be apart. Three months had nearly killed him. Dominic ground his back molars together for a moment to calm his nerves. "How is the baby?"

"Kenny is fine, fat and happy."

"Good." Dominic nodded. Prior to his father dying, Dominic had never thought about settling down with a ring. Now? He wanted a wife. He didn't want to die alone with what little family he had left hating him. A lump formed in the back of his throat with the idea. He refused to get choked up over a man like that. "Did I mention I am pleased to hear you're singing? You have a beautiful voice."

"Thank you," Waverly said as she propped her elbow on the table and covered her smile by resting her chin in her hand. "Since I don't see your name on the revised agenda, I'm guessing Anson didn't have time."

I bet, Dominic thought bitterly. "Tell me about these Advent calendars. What can I do to help?" But Dominic began too late. Mayor Ascot entered the room dressed in a dark suit with a flashy Christmas tie instead of his usual ascot. Some of the ladies at Miss Annie's table gushed at the sight. *Are you kidding me?* Dominic thought.

"Ladies and gentlemen," Ascot started. "What can I say? We survived Thanksgiving and Black Friday, and our Small Business Saturday brought in quite the crowd of out of towners. Good job and congratulations."

A round of applause broke out.

Anson calmed everyone down by lowering his hands in a repetitive motion. "Since we've held off on the holiday decorations, with the exception of the lights on Main Street for the shoppers, I'm sure everyone is ready to get started with their own Christmas decorations. We have a lot of items on the agenda today. We've got to discuss where to put the town tree."

Dominic had a nice suggestion. He would suggest shoving it right up the mayor's ass.

"We've got the neighborhood-decorating contest and we need to decide if we're going to allow entries who used the services of Macy Cuomo-Rodriguez's Winter Wonderland."

Someone in the back of the room coughed and, beneath that cough, said a name, "Rhonda."

The accused woman named Rhonda sat at a table beside Dominic and Waverly's. She stood up with her hands on her hips and faced the room. A stack of bracelets jingled as she turned to face her accusers. "Y'all can't prove I didn't decorate my house."

"You've kept your porch lights off the week before Thanksgiving," someone shouted from the back of the room. "And the day after Thanksgiving, all of a sudden your place is lit up."

Waverly leaned in to Dominic. "Winter Wonderland does all the holiday decorating over South Georgia and North Florida," she explained. "And to enter your house with Macy's designs is like rigging the amateur decorating." Macy Cuomo-Rodriguez was a professional Christmas decorator who dolled up the outsides and insides of the homes of people who lacked the vision or time to do so themselves.

"I see," Dominic said with a nod. "Do you decorate?"

Waverly nodded. "Not like I'd want to. The condo has limited space. But my balcony is going to be on point."

Good thing she is still at the condo, Dominic thought. His brothers were coming soon. Dominic had it in his mind to have a decorating party at the ranch. Waverly needed to come.

Rhonda began to clap her hands at the one accuser in the back in order to silence him. Anson had to bang his gavel. "Let's get back to order. We'll take a vote later on, maybe meet next week. Right now I'd like to go ahead and change some things around on the agenda."

Finally, Dominic thought. Maybe Anson was going to come through with adding him.

"We have our local celebrity here with us today,"

Anson said, holding his arm out toward Dominic's table…or more or less at Waverly. "Our very own Miss Southwood, Waverly Leverve."

With her hand in the air, Waverly turned and waved like a true beauty queen. "Thank you, Mayor, but you really don't have to single me out every time I attend."

"I just want you to know it's our pleasure to you have you here, Miss Southwood," the mayor gushed. "We know your time is precious and I'm hoping no one has any objections to allowing Miss Southwood to go first."

"It's really not necessary," Waverly said with a red tint to her cheeks.

"Well, okay, we'll continue with the agenda as regularly planned." The way Anson cut his eyes in Dominic's direction told him the mayor hadn't planned on letting him speak today. Thank God for his secret weapon.

The council continued on. Dominic listened to everyone vote on who would be on the judging panel. Miss Annie made it. Some of the ladies at her table got on to the food committee, which sat at the judging table for the Christmas cookie contest held at the elementary school. Southwood Middle School would host the Christmas dance for kids and then the adults would get a dance at the Southwood High.

"And now we get to hear from Miss Southwood." Anson inclined his head toward Waverly. He stepped aside for her to join him at the podium, something Dominic noticed the mayor did not do for the other presenters.

Waverly gave Dominic a slight wink as she rose from her seat but didn't move toward the stage. "Hi, everyone." She gave a friendly wave with both hands.

Everyone greeted Waverly with a round of applause.

"I don't want take up too much of your time. I just wanted to remind everyone about the donations of your services and goods for the girls at Grits and Glam Studios. The proceeds will help send everyone to the pageant in the spring. Friday is December 1. Grits and Glam is ready to sell the 3-D Southwood Advent Calendars. Most of you have already turned in goodies but I'm missing a few days for a hundred calendars." Waverly paused for a moment to peer around the room. Judging from the bowed heads, it was easy to decipher who was slacking. "I would love to have everything complete by the time I leave this evening."

Dominic sat back in amazement at the list Waverly had placed on his table. Several companies were listed. He assumed the ones with a black check mark had already fulfilled their promises. He was impressed. He scanned the list of businesses she'd collected from already: coupons for The Scoop, movie passes for the drive-in theater and the indoor theater, and enough other discounts to make up the twenty-four-day countdown.

"If y'all don't mind," Waverly began, "I have one more thing to introduce."

"By all means," said the mayor.

"Good," said Waverly. "I'd like to introduce, or maybe reintroduce, Dominic Crowne."

"Oh, look," Anson said drily, "it's Mr. Waverly, Miss Southwood's handmaiden."

The applause Dominic received wasn't as loud as Waverly's, but at least it was something that covered up the mayor's remarks. Waverly continued, "I am guessing there was a mistake in Dominic not being on the agenda, so I thought I'd share my time with him. You all may like his idea for the parade."

Dominic took his cue and rose to his feet. Like Waverly, he spoke from his table. He gave his speech about the antique cars he recently acquired whose dates of manufacture stretched all the way back to the twenties, which would add authenticity to the parade and the wardrobes. And with Dominic hiring drivers, the townspeople would be able to enjoy more of the Southwood through the decades. He waited with bated breath for some form of reaction. Kenzie started the slow clap of approval. Relieved, Dominic nodded his head in thanks at Waverly.

"This is a perfect idea with our theme." Kenzie, short in stature but with a big voice, made her way to the podium. "And great timing, too. I've got a few couples from out of town who heard about Waverly's idea and want to donate. If my calculations are right, we'll have clothes from the Civil War."

"Oh my God, Kenzie!" Waverly cheered.

"I'm glad you think so, Miss Southwood," Kenzie said with a wink. "Can I pull you away from your pageant duties to pick them up?"

Waverly shook her head. "Kenzie," she drawled the name with her Southern accent, "you do remember I still get lost in town."

The comment drew friendly giggles and nods, agreeing with Waverly's statement. A few people called out a few times and places they'd had to set Waverly on the right path. The best idea came to mind for Dominic. He would be willing to take her wherever she needed to go.

"If it's driving around town yourself," Ascot began, but Kenzie quieted him down by pressing her folder against his chest. "I bet with Dominic back, he can take over bringing Miss Southwood to her appearances, and you can focus on your job in city hall," Kenzie said to the politician. "It's a win-win situation, don't you think, Mayor?"

At that moment Dominic wanted to pull Kenzie off the stage and swing her around in joy. By the time the meeting ended, everyone clapped Dominic on the back and welcomed him back into the Southwood fold. It was nice feeling: like a hero. He finally belonged somewhere. *Take that, John Crowne.*

When the meeting was officially over, Waverly finished up collecting the coupons from the members from the Commerce of Business. She accepted their donations and apologies and placed everything in its appropriate folder. All she had to do was put the calendars in their boxes. Perhaps she'd overachieved by making 3-D replicas of downtown Southwood. Twenty-four boxes were spread out around the picture of town. She'd spent all summer and fall getting the orders perfected. Thank God she had nothing to do tomorrow.

Waverly headed over to the table with the refreshments and selected one of Miss Annie's cookies shaped as Scottish terriers dressed in Christmas sweaters. A smudge of red icing smeared against the side of her index finger. Waverly debated what to do next: lick the icing off her finger and risk getting icing from the cookie on her nose, or use her common sense and set her binder on the table with the rest of the food.

"I would pay you any amount of money to lick the icing off your finger or any body part."

Feeling his breath against the back of her neck was

enough to make Waverly lose her appetite. She set the cookie down on the top napkin of a stack and did the deed of getting the icing off herself. The sound of Anson's guttural growl evoked the image of an Elvis lip curl. "Go away, Anson."

"Do you know how eligible I am?" Anson asked, walking around to face Waverly.

In truth, Anson would be considered a handsome man. Some women went for the clean-cut, all-American guy.

"I'm well aware," Waverly responded with a yawn. She didn't need to hear his credentials again. It was unfortunate he couldn't take the hint. "And I hope for Christmas you get someone who truly values you."

Anson leaned his hip against the long table. The ice cubes in the crystal punch bowl jingled in the red liquid. "What I really want is you."

"Can you please not do this here?" Waverly asked, hugging her binder close to her chest.

"What?" Anson actually had the nerve to act surprised. His eyes lit up, and his brows rose. "Where would you like to do this? On a date?"

"No, thank you," Waverly answered quickly.

"We have a good time when we're together, Waverly."

"*You* have a great time showing me off like a bauble," Waverly clarified once more.

"The Christmas dance for the grown-ups is the twenty-second. What do you say we go together? 'The Mayor and the Beauty Queen' makes for a nice headline, don't you think?"

Anson advanced. Waverly refused to be intimidated by his nonverbal threat. She was about to square her shoulders when a set of beefy hands pressed down on hers and spun her around. Dominic's cocky grin spread before he dipped his head and pressed his lips against hers. Unlike the kiss last night outside his garage, this was friendlier—a peck or even a soft press of lips against hers. And she wanted more.

Dominic pulled away. His finger touched a spot just under her lip where she figured her lipstick might have smeared.

"Excuse me?" Anson asked, oblivious of what he'd just said to her just before Dominic came to her rescue. "While I understand you played handmaiden a few months ago for Miss Southwood, are you trying to get her kicked off the pageant circuit for violating the morality clause?"

Remembering they weren't alone, Waverly stepped beside Dominic, somehow melting into the crook of his arm. Dominic wrapped his arm around her in a protective manner. For a moment she thought he was giving Anson a thumbs-up, but she followed Anson's glance to the ceiling above them.

"Mistletoe. It is tradition." Dominic explained. "I'd get that checked out, Anson."

Anson's dark eyes narrowed on Dominic. Waverly practically felt his rage vibrate on the thin gray carpeted floor. "What am I supposed to get checked out?"

"Your slow response to things." Dominic sighed. He slipped his hand into his pocket and extracted a business card. "Dr. Rayland is the best CTE doc around."

"What?"

"Chronic traumatic encephalopathy, Anson." Dominic pressed his forefinger to his temple. "I understand you played a lot of football in your day. Maybe you should get it checked out."

Stiffening, Anson shook his head. He crumpled the card in his large hands. "What makes you think I need him?"

"Well, for starters, you overlooked the email request I sent to you—" Dominic shook his head "—and then you didn't even take advantage of the mistletoe with this beautiful woman standing underneath it."

Waverly, smitten with Dominic, stood by wordlessly. The peck was friendly and innocent enough but still hinted at the underlying desire still bubbling between them. She had so many things to say and just as she opened her mouth, she was called up to the podium. Dominic offered her a wink as she apologetically walked away.

Chapter 8

The morning after the council meeting, Waverly woke up with a stretch. It wasn't until sometime after midnight she'd fallen asleep. Every time she'd closed her eyes she felt Dominic's lips against hers. Her body ached for his touch again. Hell, had Kenzie not interrupted them last night, Waverly could have easily been talked into going home with him—Morality Committee be damned.

She checked the time on her cell phone and slipped out of bed. In her fuzzy pink slippers and white nightgown, Waverly went toward the bathroom for her morning routine. Afterward, she got into a pair of shredded pale denim shorts, a red-and-white-striped shirt and one of her favorite tiaras she'd won when she was switched from toddler to teen pageants.

Waverly headed into the kitchen for a cup of coffee.

Though the two-bedroom condo belonged to Lexi, Waverly had started to make the place home. Funny how when Waverly first came to Southwood, it was to hide from the world, but now she was invested in the community.

Something was missing in the condo. Waverly glanced around the spotless room. About fifty more calendars were spread out conveyor-belt-style for Waverly to assemble today. Then she realized there was a lack of coffee smell filling the air. She headed into the small kitchen area and sighed in despair. The green lights of the microwave flashed an odd time. From the numbers she gathered the power had gone out four hours ago, which meant her automatic coffee maker didn't go off. There was no way she could finish the project without a cup of brew.

The spacious living room with the long ivory curtains drawn open gave the perfect view of downtown Southwood. Green wires spilled out of a box, and with the breeze flowing in from the balcony, red and green reflections of the bulbs were splayed across the white carpet. Now that the Thanksgiving holidays were over, she was officially able to start decorating her balcony.

A knock came at the door at the same time her cell phone buzzed. Her mother's face appeared on the phone screen. Waverly grinned to herself. She loved that picture of her mother as a beauty queen in her teens. Waverly slid the button over to answer the call.

"Well, I was beginning to worry," said Jillian in her cool voice.

"Hi, Ma." Waverly sighed and lifted herself on tiptoe to peek through the peephole. Her eyes met the emblem of an animated smiling cup of coffee. No one bearing coffee could be dangerous.

"You took a while to answer the phone."

"It rang three times," said Waverly. She opened the door and gasped at the sight of Dominic standing in front of her, coffee in his large hand. "Oh my God, you're my savior."

Waverly accepted the hot cup and opened the door wider. It wasn't like he hadn't been in her condo before, yet a feeling of nervousness washed over her. Waverly cocked her head to the side for a glimpse of his butt. He wore a pair of his signature jeans, the kind that hugged every muscle of his legs, and a thin T-shirt, this one red.

"Waverly." Jillian's voice came to life on the other end of the line. "Waverly, what's going on?"

"Nothing, Ma." Waverly shook her head to focus on the woman who gave her birth. "I have company."

"Who is coming by this early in the morning?"

"A coffee god, Ma."

Dominic, making a beeline to the kitchen, laughed. No surprise at his familiarity. His sister's place had the same layout. Beeps sounded from the microwave and soon the flashing stopped. Waverly chuckled at his take-charge demeanor.

"Waverly, wait. First you blow off coming home for Thanksgiving last weekend..." her mother began.

"I am home," Waverly clarified and cut her off. The argument between her and her mother was growing old. Jillian expected Waverly to run to her parents every time there was something wrong. Well, now there was nothing wrong, and her mother still had a problem. Had Waverly gone home, Jillian would have paraded her around town. She'd had enough of this campaigning in her pageant region for the runoff. Jillian suffered from understanding her daughter was grown and no longer needed her help.

"You spent the holiday eating a frozen dinner."

Her mother's voice carried over the phone into the open space of the short hall and living room. Waverly prayed Dominic didn't hear, but the questioning look on his face told her he did. "Ma." Waverly grunted. "I will call you back later."

"Wait," Jillian exclaimed. "I want to remind you that you have less than a few weeks to get your act together to win this ridiculous runoff."

"I know, Ma."

"And after that you will not have that much time to get your act together for the Miss Georgia Pageant. We need to talk about your plan to bring your weight down."

A dimple appeared at the corner of Dominic's cheek. Did he always have a dimple? Waverly blinked and tried once again to focus on her mother. "I am working out but I've got a bigger response on social media for curves. People like them."

Dominic nodded in appreciation.

"You think?" Jillian's high-pitched voice reeked of sarcasm. "Or do you think you're winning over a group of people who want to see beauty pageants turn into a contact sport? Had I known you even won Miss Southwood rather than finding out through social media about that and your brawl—"

"Listen, Ma." Waverly interrupted quickly. "I've got to go. I promise I'm going to call you later." She hung up before her mother gave another embarrassing detail or guilted Waverly for not telling her about winning Miss Southwood.

"You didn't go home for the holidays?" Dominic asked, coming from behind the counter. Waverly willed her feet to bring her closer into the split living room. She watched quietly while Dominic strolled over to the balcony. He bent over to examine the box of lights and decorations.

"Southwood is my home," Waverly answered, closing the gap between them. "Thanks again for the coffee."

"Two sugars and the sugar cookie creamer you mentioned you liked."

Waverly blinked in disbelief.

"I remembered because you went on about the flavors of coffee on our date." Dominic tried to recover. The sun caught a slight blush on his cheeks. "I remember thinking the flavor of coffee should be…coffee."

Playfully rolling her eyes as if she were annoyed, Waverly motioned toward the cream-colored couch. How could anyone be annoyed with a man like him bringing her a much-needed brew? "That wasn't a date—we were celebrating my win."

"Our win," he corrected her. Dominic glanced down at his attire before sitting. "So how'd you know I'd need coffee?"

"Alisha came to the garage late this morning," Dominic said. "She swore being late today was not her fault and mentioned the blackout before I started to fire her. Are these your only decorations?"

So much for family loyalty, Waverly thought with a frown. "Were you going to fire her?"

"I was tempted," said Dominic as he stood up with the box in his arms. It was too light for the bulge of his biceps to emerge, so Waverly was pretty sure he was showing off for her. "This is sad," he said with a quick shake of his head. "Maybe while we're out today we can pick up some decent decorations."

Waverly sat down adjacent to Dominic. Her bare knees touched his jeans-clad ones. No barrier between them stopped the heat rising. "Why do you think we're going out today?"

"Because Kenzie sent a message to us to pick up some dresses," said Dominic.

Flipping the phone over in her hand, Waverly checked for the mail icon and found it. Kenzie's name appeared by the envelope. "Well, I guess she did."

"I figured you were ready." He pointed at the tiara on top of her head. "What are you going to do for a tree?"

"I have a picture of a tree I'm going to hang up on the wall. As a matter of fact, it should be folded up in the box."

Dominic shook his head and hung it low. Waverly wondered what he did to keep his curls looking so soft. She refrained from touching the top of his head. She hated it when she was in pageant mode and someone wanted to touch her bouffant.

"My Christmas spirit weeps for you." Dominic glanced up. The light caught his brown eyes, turning them copper.

"Speaking of Christmas, I really like the way you're treating the town with your cars so everyone can enjoy the parade. I didn't realize you owned so many." Waverly sat back into the cushions, crossing one leg over the other, well aware of Dominic's eyes on her. She cleared her throat and he glanced up, making eye contact. Waverly's heart fluttered, not sure which she'd rather have more: him staring at her legs or looking into her eyes.

"Let's just say I came into a fleet." Dominic's jaw twitched. "I don't think I won over Mayor Ascot."

"Anson," Waverly corrected him with a smirk. "I know you know his name."

"He didn't seem too pleased about me honoring the mistletoe tradition." Dominic teased her with an enticing side smile.

"Honoring tradition." She scoffed, hoping her snark would stop the blush threatening. "Is that what you call it?"

Dominic's shoulders rose and fell. "So, do I need to be worried?"

"Worried about what?" Waverly asked.

"According to what Kenzie told me, you've just about collected all decades of clothing for your idea."

"Begging for donations at five county fairs, fifty football homecomings, twenty hospitals and the thirty or so senior citizen homes worked." Waverly relaxed against the cushions of the couch after stating her recollection. "What do you have to be worried about?"

"You won't need me."

Need or want? Waverly asked inwardly. "I'll admit I've been busy."

Being busy had helped keep her mind off Dominic's absence. But he didn't need to know that.

"So I need to make sure the amount of time we spend together counts," Dominic explained. "Let's see… Tomorrow is the first, so we've got twenty-five days together, spending time to create the perfect parade."

Waverly's mouth twisted into a crooked smile. Twenty-five days of Dominic? Her heart raced with excitement. "Providing you don't have to leave again."

"I'm not going anywhere."

"That's right," Waverly said, "you've got this Kris Kringle thing going."

Dominic nodded and answered quickly, "Yep." He stood up and stretched. Waverly found herself licking her lips, enthralled with the shape of his body in his clothes. She could only imagine what he looked like with them off. "So, are you ready to get going?"

"What do you mean?"

Dominic pointed toward her phone. "We've got to go pick up some dresses. Kenzie's orders, remember?"

"Where are we going?"

"Someplace across the county line," Dominic said with a shrug. "We can catch lunch there and then, when we get back, if you don't mind, I'd like to help you get your Advent calendars together."

Waverly tilted her head to the side. She'd like that… she'd like it very much.

"This is some spread," Dominic said and whistled when they pulled up to the curb of address Kenzie provided them. He stepped around the black 1940 Packard and opened the door for Waverly. Like any other red-blooded American man's would, his eyes went toward her legs. Waverly had changed into a knee-length tan skirt and an orange sweater with a collar that teased him with a hint of her shoulders. The skirt rose just to her thighs when she turned in her seat to set her tan heels on the ground. Wind cooled his bottom lip, which he absentmindedly licked at the sight of her stems.

"Oh my God, this place is gorgeous." Waverly's eyes lit up as she took in the structure. "When I retire from the pageant world, I want to own a place like this and raise a family."

Dominic gave her a wink and took mental note of her dream house. The Italian Renaissance revival house reeked of living history. From the outside of the redbrick home, it appeared to have at least four floors. But given Dominic's love for history and the age of the house, he was willing to bet on a few extra nonvisible floors. He secretly hoped the Harveys would give them a tour of the mansion. Dominic was dying to get a look at the cupola, the white dome with a gold cap that topped the flat roof. This was one of the many things Dominic loved about living in Georgia. It was so rich with the past. An American flag swayed in the wind high up on the flagpole. He wondered if a rebel flag had ever hung from it. He wouldn't have been surprised.

The dark pine double doors opened and an older, dark-skinned African American man stepped out first, dressed in Civil War Union Blues. A half second later, a pleasantly plump woman in a patchwork dress followed. Her gloved hands went to her mouth and her eyes widened with what seemed to be excitement.

"Welcome," the two chorused.

Waverly reached for Dominic's hand. Her little fingers curled around the side of his hand. "Here we go," she said under her breath. Glancing down, Dominic watched as she transformed herself from the slouch in the passenger seat to a full-fledged beauty queen, seven-inch tiara included.

"Mr. and Mrs. Harvey." Waverly greeted the elderly couple with a strong, boisterous, peppy voice. Her smile, causing her eyes to crinkle in the corners, spread across her face. "Thank you so much for having us."

"Oh, we're so blessed to have you," said Mrs. Harvey, stepping down off her wraparound porch. "Please,

I'm Fannie, and this is my husband, Stan. We know you two are probably on a tight schedule and want to get back on the road, but we hope you'll stay for lunch."

"Considering your sizable donation, we'd be willing to spend the night." Waverly laughed.

"Really?" Fannie asked eagerly. "We can have the fourth floor set up for the two of you."

"Fourth?" Waverly repeated. "I only counted two levels."

Once they climbed the dozen or so wide front porch steps, Stan held the doors open for the two of them to enter. Everyone's footsteps sounded off the hardwood floors of the porch and changed in pitch when they all entered the marble hallway. Dominic tried not to gasp in awe too much.

"You look like a man who appreciates historic things," said Mr. Harvey, slapping him on the back. "I can tell by the car you're driving. Packard?"

"Yes, sir," Dominic confirmed with a nod. "It's been a project of mine."

Waverly placed her hand on Dominic's forearm. He felt her pride as she spoke about his profession. "Dominic restores old cars. Maybe you've heard of his company? Crowne's Garage?"

Mr. Harvey's mouth twisted as he nodded. "Yep, your name is well known in my circle of friends. I see you're missing your winged goddess."

Dominic turned and sighed at the missing hood ornament. "Yes, I'm in search of one."

"I might know some folks who can help out." Stan left his hand on Dominic's shoulder. "You're a big fellow, ain't you? Ever thought of doing some reenacting?"

"I'm sorry, what?" Dominic leaned closer to make sure he'd heard correctly.

"Fannie and I are Civil War reenactors," he said, glancing down at himself. "We have a speaking engagement after lunch."

Good to know. Dominic was worried they dressed like this on a day-to-day basis.

"We could always use a strong guy like yourself," Stan went on. "And I'm sure one of my friends might be able to help you out with your missing ornament."

Ahead of the men, Waverly cast a glance over her right shoulder and gave Dominic a slight smile. "Please say you'll do it."

Dominic scratched the back of his neck. He was willing to give and do anything for Waverly, but dressing up and playing soldier? He'd have to think twice. Thankfully Fannie Harvey filled the short walk into the formal sitting room with the history of the house.

Mrs. Fannie Harvey led them down the main level, or *proper* level, as she explained. During a light lunch of crustless pimento cheese sandwiches and sweet tea, she gave them a history lesson about their home's changes of hands over the years. The house once belonged to a man named George Harvey, Stan's great-grandfather. He was born before the Civil War and raised as a slave but served in the house because the owner was his biological father. When the war broke out, the white owners, the Harveys, were allowed to sit out and send their slaves as their representatives. George went to war and survived. When he returned, the Harveys had sold off the rest of his family in order to maintain their lifestyle. George headed down to Southwood and married a nice woman. When he turned sixty-nine, World War I broke out and the original Harveys put their home up for sale. This was not an uncommon event for a lot of families who stayed in the South. The structure didn't sell until the stock market crashed ten years later. George gathered all his and his family's money together and purchased the building for a sweet price. The Harveys had been passing down their home from generation to generation.

"And with our kids all grown and on the verge of being on their own once they find jobs," Fannie finished, "we've just been finding things around here to give to good homes."

"We'd seen you, Waverly, serving the veterans on Thursday," Stan said. "And it stuck with us."

"That, and you look so much like George's mother, Sissy Harvey." Fannie reached in the folds of her skirt and extracted a silver locket. She opened the tiny lock and showed Waverly and Dominic the old grainy black-and-white photo of a woman and man filling the circular space.

Waverly's mouth opened wide. "She does look like we could be some kin. I'll have to ask my mother what she knows."

Dominic peered over his glass of tea at Waverly. She sat with her elbows on the table, enthralled with the story. She was so animated at every bit of detail. Fannie pushed the locket close to Dominic's face.

"Interesting," he said. The image favored Waverly with her dark hair and large oval eyes.

A grandfather clock chimed noon. Waverly sighed and rose to her feet. Everyone stood with her. "I can't thank y'all enough for sharing your history with us."

Dominic glanced at his phone and noted a storm was predicted to hit Southwood before nightfall. Fannie and Stan bade the two of them goodbye, waving them off and watching as Dominic secured the outfits in the trunk of the car. Waverly sat in her passenger seat with her legs crossed and had never looked sexier.

"Why did you allow your mother to think you were alone for Thanksgiving?" Dominic asked Waverly as he pulled the old car onto the road. "Serving vets was a prime opportunity for the pageant board to see you in your element."

Beside him, Waverly shrugged. "According to my mother, if the cameras aren't on, it's not worth it." She sighed heavily and twisted her slender hands together in her lap.

Dominic gripped the steering wheel tighter. Proud of himself, he owed himself a beer for behaving right now. Didn't Waverly realize what a temptation she was? "Your mom sounds, ah, interesting," he said for lack of a better word. He couldn't say what truly came to mind: *controlling* and *domineering*.

"I'm her only daughter," Waverly said. "I've gone further in the pageant circuit than she has, and so I believe she's living vicariously through me."

"Serving veterans as a regular person instead of as Miss Southwood wouldn't please her?" Dominic asked, cutting his eyes over.

"In Jillian's book, anything other than pageanting is pathetic, especially with the runoff coming up." Waverly flashed him a sly smile. "I serve because it's the right thing to do. I didn't ask for publicity like Vera did down in Savannah. My father was in the Marines.

I knew I'd be by myself this holiday. When I started feeling sorry for myself, I thought about all the soldiers away from family. I had to go down and serve. The lunch was for them, not to spotlight me."

The distant sound of imaginary wedding bells rang through his ears. Dominic couldn't wait for this pageant crap to be over with. Concentrating on the road, he took the exit leading north. Waverly cocked her head at him.

"We have one more stop before I bring you home," Dominic explained.

Waverly's large brown eyes widened. "What kind of stop?"

"I'm getting you a proper Christmas tree for your place."

Dominic veered off the interstate toward a sign offering the state's best trees. This morning his strict instructions had been to take Waverly upstate to the Harveys' and get the wardrobe. Mission accomplished.

"I really don't need a tree," Waverly argued.

"Sure you do. Let's go."

The lot allowed people to come and chop down their own trees once they found the right one. He pretended to allow Waverly to decide what kind she wanted, and she at last chose wisely with each frown he gave. Finally Waverly picked the right one and Dominic got the chance to show off his brawny skills by chopping down the tree and bringing it back to the car. However, he had to eat crow when they drove down the road a bit and the tree slid off the roof as Dominic swerved to avoid hitting a deer.

"Far be it from me to be the one to say I told you so," Waverly said as she leaned her tan-skirt-clad hip against the side of the Packard. Before they left the parking lot, Waverly strongly suggested he cross the ties for a securer hold. But he knew what he was doing. She pressed her lips together to keep from actually saying, "I told you so."

A spot of black grease was streaked across Dominic's face. The sun had long ago sank and the moon had appeared. "You're lucky you're cute."

Waverly batted her lashes. "And I am an able body, too. Please let me help."

"I've got this." Dominic grunted and spun the wheel of his iron to change the tire. "You can help me when my brothers come to town and it's time to decorate the tree."

For a moment she imagined a Christmas tree at Dominic's house decorated with spark plugs and lug nuts. She recalled the photo of the twins from Dominic's wallet the first night they kissed. Heat rose from her collarbone from the memory. *Focus on something else*, Waverly willed herself. Not the way Dominic's muscles rippled in the moonlight. For some reason, changing a tire meant having to take off his shirt. Not like she was complaining. Dominic's shirtless frame was a sight for sore eyes. The man was a sculpted god.

Waverly cleared her throat. "When are they coming?"

"Probably in a week or so, when school gets out," said Dominic. The wheel came loose and he made the change while he talked about Alisha taking classes in the spring. Waverly thought about the things she was going to miss as she focused on Miss Georgia. Listening to the Harveys today had left Waverly's heart heavy. She wanted that kind of love, the kind that transcended history. But time wasn't on Waverly's side. The runoff, Miss Georgia and then Miss USA were right at her fingertips. Did she expect Dominic to wait that long?

Waverly turned her head to the side and watched the muscles in Dominic flex. He cursed and grunted but finally got the old tire changed out to the new one. Pine needles were scattered across the top of the car. From the incident, the road rash had resulted in a half-bare tree.

Standing, Dominic wiped his hands on the back of his jeans. His six-pack abs flexed and Waverly averted her eyes toward the tree. The timber was safe from getting run over, thanks to the back road Dominic had thought to take. His eyes followed hers. "I'm getting you another tree. We're tossing this."

Before he took another step toward the road, Waverly reached for Dominic's arm. His biceps twitched beneath her palm. "I don't need a tree."

Dominic paused for a moment. Their eyes locked. Suddenly the tree was no longer in question. Waverly's heart raced. Her feelings, jumbled with the longing for what the Harveys had and wanting it with Dominic, came to mind.

"What is it you need, Waverly?"

"I—I—" The words were lost but the action was not. Waverly leaped forward and threw herself into Dominic's arms. He caught her and spun her body around, placing her back against the car. Waverly gave him a further answer with a kiss. Her mouth pressed against his, searching and finding that same desire she felt each time they touched.

He yanked her skirt up her thighs. The material

rolled farther up when he pulled her legs around his waist. Waverly moaned and broke the kiss, turning her face toward the sky. Dominic kissed her chin, earlobes and neck, and then nuzzled the valley between her breasts. Skillfully Dominic balanced Waverly's body against his, pressing her back to the door while his fingers crept up her thigh and between her legs. The fabric of her panties was now moist with blatant desire. Unabashed, Waverly rolled her hips forward. Dominic slid beneath the cotton fabric from the side and pressed one finger inside her.

"Jesus," Dominic whispered. "I'm not going to be able to stop."

"So don't."

The single word evoked a husky grunt. Dominic lifted Waverly in his arms and reached for his shirt, hanging from the door, then carried her over to the hood. Waverly placed several kisses across Dominic's neck as he maneuvered around. He set her down. She realized he'd placed his shirt under her so her bare behind wouldn't touch the cold car. Waverly bit the bottom corner of her lip and watched Dominic step backward. His belt buckle jingled in the air when he slipped his pants over his hips. His black boxer briefs slid down, and in the dim light a foil package of protection glinted. Waverly's heart jumped with anticipation. She pulled her feet up onto the hood of the car. The height of the vehicle made it perfect for Dominic to hit his target. With one deep stroke he entered her. They both gasped.

Waverly rolled her head back. Dominic feasted on her neck, earlobes and chin, and then cupped the back of her head and brought her mouth to his. In these woods, stranded on the side of the road and with a storm approaching, Waverly had never felt more protected. This feeling she experienced, this sensation, was more than just gratuitous sex. This was deeper. This was love.

Moisture struck her face. Was she sad? Dominic's hands roamed her body. Each tender caress he gave her swelled her heart with love. Waverly shook her head and broke the kiss only to realize clouds had rolled in and covered the moon. Darkness fell on them while the rain did the same.

At the crack of thunder, Waverly was almost at her breaking point. Dominic spread her back against the car, slid her farther down on him and drove into her. With nothing to grip while her first orgasm broke, Waverly dragged her fingers through her hair, pushing her tiara to the side. Dominic threw her legs over his shoulders and banged into her...until he seemingly lost his breath for a moment. Through the flashes of lightning, she saw that veins popped out in his neck and forearms. Finally he breathed and when he did, the two of them combusted into dual orgasms.

The ride down County Road 17, which brought them into town, was filled with holiday music from the radio. Waverly had no idea what to say. She wasn't filled with regret but more of a realization she'd opened up a whole can of worms. How was she going to be able to stop wanting Dominic now? Waverly distracted herself with the decorations in the suburbs, oohing and aahing with her face pressed against the window.

Dominic's hair was darkened with droplets left over from getting caught in the rain. "I'm getting you another tree."

They entered the covered parking garage to her condo instead of Dominic dropping her off at the front door for the doorman to let her in. Dominic pulled the Packard into a guest parking spot rather than the one assigned to Waverly or even his sister. Waverly wondered if that was so Alisha wouldn't question what happened tonight. The two of them were still soaking wet and it would take no guessing what they had been up to, judging from their wet clothing.

Being the gentleman that he was, Dominic opened the passenger door for Waverly. Their footsteps fell in unison along the floor of the parking garage.

"I can bring the dresses over to Lexi's in the morning," Dominic offered. Their fingers brushed together.

"Sounds good to me." Waverly pressed the up button of the elevator.

Waverly said a silent prayer for the elevator to be on a higher floor. The ding cut deep and the light from the PG sign lit up as Dominic pressed his lips together.

"Did you say something?" Waverly asked.

They stepped into the compartment. Would it be too much to ask for the elevator to get stuck?

"I'm good," he replied. "I just know if I ride in the elevator with you I can't promise to keep my hands off you."

"You," Waverly began with a mild clearing of her throat, "you understand my situation, Dominic, right?"

Dominic's eyes widened. "Seriously? After tonight, you're back to the morality thing?"

Waverly stiffened at the harsh tone. "I've been waiting all my life for this chance." As the words rolled off her tongue, Waverly wondered what the *this* was. Love or the pageant.

Without having to say a word, Dominic got his answer. He pressed his lips together and nodded. "All right."

The elevator arrived and Waverly reluctantly stepped out of the compartment. "Do you want to come in and dry off?"

"Nah," he said with a shake of his head. "I'll get those dresses over tomorrow."

Chapter 9

"These dresses are gorgeous."

Waverly craned her neck over the stack of ready Advent calendars. The top of Lexi's blond head appeared in the break room. The dresses had been dropped off before Waverly arrived at work. She hated admitting her disappointment at not being able to see Dominic again. She didn't like the way things had ended. Honestly, in her dream ending of their evening, they would have ended up in bed together. Clearing her naughty thoughts out of her mind with a shake of her head, Waverly leaned around, expecting to find the stroller with the baby prince, Kenny, inside.

"Don't look so disappointed because it's just me." Lexi frowned and then playfully poked her tongue out.

When it came time for Waverly to get serious about pageants, Jillian had made sure she had the best pageant coach ever, and that was none other than Lexi Pender-grass Reyes—at the time. Now anyone with a camera who wanted to host their own social media show could claim they were the best pageant coach.

"Aw, don't get your feelings in a bunch." Waverly laughed as she rose up from her seat. She crossed the hardwood floors of the studio in the four-inch heels she wore just to keep herself in constant training. It didn't matter that the strappy black sandals were out of place with the denim shorts and turquoise Grits and Glam Gowns and Studios shirt she wore. "I am equally glad to see you."

"Don't tell that lie." Lexi laughed. The two old friends hugged.

Lexi, graceful as ever, glided across the dance floor directly to the window. "Oh, look, the garage *is* opened."

There was nothing in Lexi's monotone voice to lead toward surprise. Waverly followed her over to the window and crossed her arms and understood Lexi's flat, teasing tone. "This is why I hate living in a small town," Waverly said with a shake of her head.

"What?" Lexi overdramatically gaped. She pressed her hand against her chest. "Are you implying that I came down here of my own free will, fueled by the gossip of the heated make-out session between you and Dominic Crowne at the Christmas Advisory Council the other night?" Lexi didn't even fool herself with the innocent act. She collapsed on the couch to sober up her laughing fit.

Waverly leaned against the cool glass. It was almost December and the weather showed no sign of changing from early fall. The air conditioner was the only thing bringing in the seasonal spirit. Last night's storm only brought in the humidity.

With the mention of Dominic, Waverly naturally cast a glance across the street. The garage doors were open. Two cars were in line to get checked out. Three workers came out to guide Miss Brittany Foley's Jaguar. She stepped out of her vehicle in a pair of way too short shorts and a leopard-print tank top. Highly inappropriate for an elementary school teacher, Waverly thought to herself. Did the trollop think she was going to get Dominic's attention like that? And where was he anyway? The several dozen times she'd already glanced out there, she hadn't seen him at all. Was he that buried in paperwork?

"Earth to Waverly," Lexi said, snapping her fingers. "You okay, girl?"

"Sorry." Waverly recovered. She rubbed her neck with her right hand and moved away from the window. Any more glances out there and she'd reach stalker level. "What brings you in today? Besides this being your own establishment?"

"Stephen was driving me nuts and the kids don't get out of school for a few more weeks. I tell ya, I got spoiled with last week's Thanksgiving break."

Lexi wasn't fooling anyone. She loved having Stephen by her side. How many days had Reyes Realty next door been run by interns or Nate, rather than the head man himself?

"I'll believe you want a break," said Waverly. She plopped down on the other end of the couch.

"Tired of being Miss Southwood?" Lexi asked. "You're about to change titles, especially now since you almost have your six months' residency in."

Waverly shook her head no. "I love being Miss Southwood, but it was nice last weekend not to have to get dressed up for anything or travel."

"Yeah, speaking of travel," Lexi said, pressing her hand against Waverly's shoulder. Waverly glanced at her friend's unmanicured nails. What a strange sight to see. Lexi was always dressed to a T, and now she sat here with an orange stain over her shoulder, a yellow splotch on her capri jeans. "You didn't come over to the house."

"Lexi, I worked at the vet center in Black Wolf Creek serving Thanksgiving food."

"Oh," Lexi cooed and reached for her phone. "I'm on an alert for any social media posts of you. Where are the photos?"

"I didn't alert anyone in the pageant circuit."

"What?" Lexi gaped. "No wonder I didn't find you. Waverly serving at a vet center would be a great photo op to upgrade your image and secure everyone's vote for the runoff."

"Nah," said Waverly. "I didn't let the committee know I was going. I just did it to go—it wouldn't seem as sincere if I had cameras following me."

"Jillian must have had a fit."

"I didn't bother telling her," Waverly said with a shrug. "When I finished in Black Wolf Creek, I came home and curled up on the couch with some fried turkey and corn bread and stuffing wontons, and I washed it all down with a cranberry smoothie while I watched the recorded parade."

"That sounds disgusting."

"The disgusting part was not even changing out of my pj's the rest of the weekend." Waverly chuckled.

"You know, I don't think I even pulled a brush through my hair until Sunday night."

Lexi rolled her eyes. "And I thought I was bad."

"You at least have a reason for looking a mess."

"Hey now." Lexi pouted and touched her blond hair. Women spent hundreds of dollars to get Lexi's color—which she came by naturally. And she never looked a mess.

Waverly leaned over and bumped Lexi's shoulder. "I'm kidding."

"Make it up to me by telling me about this heat between you and Dominic."

Absentmindedly Waverly pressed her hand to her lips. Then she panicked. Had someone told her about last night? "Huh?"

"The kiss at the Christmas Advisory Council."

"Oh, yeah." Waverly breathed a sigh of relief. "Dominic was just being nice and saved me from Anson."

The mention of the mayor's name evoked a drastic eye roll from Lexi.

"Yes, the re-emergence of Dominic Crowne sent this man into several states of insecurity," said Waverly. "Not like Anson had a chance. But you'd never know, the way he cornered me at the cookie table."

"Which one?"

"Which table?" Waverly asked.

"Which cookie?" Lexi clarified.

"Miss Annie's," Waverly answered. She decided to ask Lexi later about the little shoulder shimmy Lexi did over the cookies. One should not be so excited about a cookie. "Anyway, so Anson was going on about how we'd be such a great couple."

"Ugh."

"I know. And did you know Dominic sent him an email over the weekend, asking to be on the agenda for a few minutes, and Anson acted like he never received it?"

"Yet Dominic shared his plan for the parade and the floats?" Lexi inquired.

Waverly went on to tell Lexi about the events from yesterday with the Harveys and the Christmas tree, but made it a point not to mention anything else.

"So Dominic's back in town for twenty-four hours and you're getting all googly-eyed."

"What?" Waverly clamped her hand over her mouth to keep from laughing at Lexi's terminology. "I'm not having this conversation with you."

"So if I were Jolene, you would tell me how you wouldn't mind if he crammed his tongue down your throat?"

Jolene would get the whole tea, but she wasn't, so Waverly needed to figure things out on her own. For a bad boy, Dominic didn't appear to like leaving what happened on the side of the road for what it was—a moment in time for them. One hot, passionate moment. Beads of sweat began to gather at the nape of Waverly's neck. She lifted her long hair and twisted it into a bun at the top of her head.

"Jesus, girl." Lexi fanned Waverly's cheeks with her hand. She hopped up, jogged over to the kitchen and returned with two glasses of tea. "I haven't seen you so fevered before since... Geez, I don't know when. Who was the motorcycle boy you were in love with when you were sixteen?"

"Why you gotta bring up the past?" The sugary beverage brought down the temperature in her body.

Waverly tilted the glass further until she captured an ice cube.

"You lost your chance to compete in a pageant."

Waverly didn't need the reminder. It was her spiral down toward the big dethroning. "History won't repeat itself. The Morality Committee made quite an impression."

Even though Waverly captured another ice cube, she caught Lexi's eye roll. "The committee can't keep you from having a social life, Waverly. You just can't go out and have hot sex on the hood of a car in a park."

Waverly choked on the piece of ice in her mouth. She leaned forward and coughed.

Taking the hint, Lexi sighed and changed the subject. "Fine. Just remember what I said—you're still allowed a social life. Even when you win Miss Georgia or Miss USA, you're still going to want to have a personal life once it ends."

"Not if I go on to Miss Universe."

Lexi snatched the material from Waverly's hands. "Don't make me hurt you, girl. Don't be like me and wait until it's almost too late."

"Let me get through this runoff."

Lexi patted Waverly's thigh. "What's your plan?"

"Same as always—win."

"Just what I like to hear."

Waverly spent the rest of the afternoon welcoming in the mothers of contestants and customers of Grits and Glam Gowns and Studios. They sold every single Advent calendar as well as a few dresses. Some of Waverly's students wanted to know what was in every box, but that would have spoiled the surprise. Some of the calendars were separated into boxes for the different genders, in case one of the boys receiving a calendar protested the idea of a free pageant lesson. She was truly touched by the way the Chamber of Commerce came together to donate physical calendars in the shape of downtown Southwood.

Shenanigans, one of the popular kids' hangouts in town, offered a free pizza. Smart thinking, since no one ever left Shenanigans without ordering at least three. The Scoop offered a free cone for whenever. And the drive-in theater was going to be packed with its carload offer for a free movie. The voucher date was December 15, which was perfect timing for when school got out for the holidays. The Cupcakery offered a free cupcake and hot chocolate—only if it ever got cold enough for one.

The sun had already disappeared behind city hall when Lexi left. Andrew skipped out for a long-awaited date, which Waverly didn't mind. Chantal had headed down to central Florida and took Stephen's colleague Keenan with her. Andrew needed to be around more people. Waverly loved hanging out with him, but her duties as Miss Southwood often left him to go places stag.

The bells over the door to Grits and Glam Gowns jingled. Waverly was still in the kitchen, rinsing off a rag to get ready to wipe down the register. "We're closed," she hollered, turning off the sink. When she didn't hear a response right away, she dropped the rag, worrying it was a child wandering in from the street. She slammed into a large body—Dominic's body, to be exact.

"Hey, I saw your lights on," Dominic said, taking hold of her shoulders.

Electricity coursed through her veins. With her heels on, Waverly came just to his chin. She blinked under his dazzling smile. "I planned on turning them off in a minute once I finished wiping down the counters."

"Need any help?" Dominic peered over her head toward the sink. "Here." He stepped over to the sink and grabbed the rag. "What were you going to clean?"

"The register."

"Do you do that all the time?"

Waverly nodded slowly. "Do you know how filthy they are?"

"I work with my hands, Waverly. Everything about me is dirty 95 percent of the time."

She watched him walk over to the counter. He was careful not to touch any of the dresses, probably because of what he'd said. On his blue jeans and white T-shirt, Waverly saw no dirt. All she saw was a fine specimen of a man helping her out for the evening. Waverly finished locking the doors to the studios and met Dominic in the kitchen.

"I didn't just come over here because the lights were on," said Dominic. "I wanted to walk you home this evening."

Heart fluttering, Waverly nodded and thought about Lexi's words. They cleaned together. Dominic emptied the trash before closing.

"I know it's not far," Dominic began. He nodded toward Waverly's feet. "But do you want to change shoes before walking?"

"If I'm going to win Miss Georgia next year, I need to have these shoes glued to my feet."

"After you win the runoff?" Dominic held the door to the boutique open and took the keys from Waverly to lock up.

Waverly flashed a tight smile. "Did you lose confidence in me?"

"Never," he replied quickly. "Have you given any thought to what you would do if you didn't lose?"

"Winning the Miss Georgia tiara is the only thing I've ever wanted since I was a kid."

Before turning off the store lights, Dominic's lips pressed together. "Well, if it's a tiara you want…" Dominic said, his mouth close to her ear. He pressed the keys back into Waverly's hand. "A tiara you shall receive."

As she walked through the front door, Waverly's heart sank with wonder. Lexi's words played over in her head. Was she so focused on the pageant she wasn't seeing what was right in front of her face? Something about Dominic's tone sent a wave of worry throughout her soul. Was she too late for love?

Mr. Myers ran his liver-spotted hand over the hood of his Model K and let out a low whistle. "I can't believe you were able to fix it."

Dominic leaned his hip against the counter of the register and wiped his hands on a clean white rag. With a few days to spare, he finished the retired teacher's old car and sent his worker Billy to pick up Mr. Myers so he could drive it home today. "It's been a pleasure working on it. I'm just sorry it took so long to get it finished for you."

"Think nothing of it. This baby is going to fetch a few glances at the parade this year." Mr. Myers stopped fondling his car long enough to come over and shake Dominic's hand. "You're all right with me driving it in the parade, right? I understand you have your own set of drivers for your cars."

"Sure." Dominic beamed. "I don't want to exclude anyone."

Mr. Myers elbowed Dominic in the ribs. "I'm dying to come out to your place and get a look."

"What are you doing next weekend?"

The wrinkles on Mr. Myers's face deepened. "Hopefully the widow Mrs. Huggins."

"I believe Mrs. Huggins is dating Ralph, the pianist from the Methodist church." As Dominic spoke, he realized he knew way too much about the town's gossip.

Puffing out his chest, Mr. Myers shook his head and spoke. "If I know I can beat up the boyfriend, she's single in my eyes."

Dominic pinched the bridge of his nose to keep from laughing. And he needed to laugh. It had been two days since he and Waverly crossed the line. Their conversation yesterday was probably the most awkward they'd ever had. But he needed the distance. The last thing he wanted was to come between Waverly and her crown. In his absence Waverly accomplished a lot. She was focused and winning in the silly social media polls. He couldn't help but wonder if him not being around had a lot to do with it. Since he would never be able to abide by the moral codes when it came to Waverly and her body, the best thing to do was leave her alone.

Mr. Myers cleared his throat. "What do you say we head over to your place and check them out now?"

Dominic scratched the back of his neck. How did he tell this man he was at work? But then again, he was the boss. "Billy?"

Billy, Miss Annie's grandson, poked his head out from under the hood of a car getting an oil change. "Yeah, boss?"

"Mr. Myers and I are going to run out to my ranch," Dominic announced. He shrugged out of his overalls. No grease or grime smeared his khaki pants or the light blue polo shirt with Crowne scripted on the pocket. Alisha insisted the garage workers needed to wear matching shirts.

"Fine by me, boss."

Dominic tossed the keys to Mr. Myers. "Feels good to have these back in my hands again."

They both got in the car at the same time. Mr. Myers went on about his baby purring. This was the part of Dominic's job that he loved the most. It wasn't about collecting old cars, finding them or even selling them. It was about bringing a car together with its owner. He thought about the confidence he restored in Waverly. Had he known helping her become Miss Southwood would result in them not being together, he might not have taken the job.

The afternoon sun warmed Dominic's face. The fickle Southern weather couldn't decide what season it wanted to be. Today crispness lingered in the air. With the temperature finally beginning to change, it made the holiday season a reality. At the sound of the tires squealing at a sharp left turn, Dominic gripped the side of the door.

"Everything okay?" he asked Mr. Myers.

"Oh, yeah, sure, sure." He chuckled. "I just remembered the news mentioned the Elder Elf list went up today. Mind if we stop by? It's right down Sunshine Street."

Considering Mr. Myers halted the freshly restored vehicle a half inch in front of someone's gold Cadillac and turned off the ignition, Dominic shook his head no. "What is Elder Elf?"

"This here's the Senior Citizen Center." Mr. Myers gave off a lecherous laugh. "Where I like to shop."

A cement ramp built beside a set of stairs led up to a redbrick three-story building. Two empty walkers stood at the top of the ramp. Dominic looked around for the owners and prayed no one had fallen. He didn't see anyone. Red and gold garlands festooned the arched doorway and a giant decorated wreath hung from a hook. A red picket fence outlined a green manicured lawn. Mr. Myers was out of his side of the car within seconds and halfway up the stairs before Dominic got out.

"So the Elder Elf Helper happens every year," Mr. Myers began, waiting for Dominic to catch up. "Every Christmas, a list goes out here requesting help with some of the older folks."

The word *older* played in Dominic's mind. Mr. Myers was pushing seventy. What was old to him? "So you like to help?" Dominic asked his question when they reached the top step.

"Every Christmas I get first dibs at the list of the eligible women who need help with things. Sometimes it's someone to take them to dinner. Sometimes it's taking them around to go shopping. Now, with my baby back, I'm in business for some smooching time and none of the ladies can get mad at me for two-timing."

"You old coot." Dominic chuckled.

They each reached for one of the handles of the double doors. Dominic wasn't sure what he expected, but it wasn't the roaring party going on in the room immediately to the left. A crowd of scrubs-wearing helpers stood peering inside. Mr. Myers pulled Dominic around the crowd and got them an empty spot to stand by the front window. Red and green construction paper cut out in interconnected rings decorated a large evergreen propped in the corner by an empty fireplace. On the other side of the chimney stood a folding table covered in a snowman tablecloth and filled with cookies stacked in a pyramid. A jug of apple juice stood by a tower of nine-ounce paper cups. At twelve in the afternoon, the party was in full swing.

An older gentleman wearing a page boy cap sat at a piano tickling the keys to a catchy Christmas tune. A crowd of people gathered around the baby grand, singing along to "The Twelve Days of Christmas." When the five golden rings part came, the voice of an angel belted out. Dominic's heart thumped.

"Waverly," he breathed. Her sweet voice evoked devilish thoughts. And he needed to stay away from her, why?

Dominic hung back and waited for the song to end. The crowd parted. Perched on the table was the vision of beauty. Waverly wore a red sequined dress with a slit up to her thigh. Her hair was blown straight and covered her left eye in an old-fashioned forties style. The old men in the room gawked at her. The women all clapped and cheered for Waverly.

"Well, ladies and gentlemen," Waverly said, "what do you say we take a break?" She was met with a round of boos, but Mr. Myers stepped forward and inquired about the list for Elder Elves. Gray-haired ladies surrounded him, giving Waverly a chance to escape.

"Dominic, hi," Waverly said breathlessly. The ten-inch crown she wore today was highlighted with faux diamonds and gold. "What brings you here?"

Dominic pointed in the direction of the ladies' man. "Mr. Myers wanted to come out to my ranch and got sidetracked when he realized this infamous list came out today."

"The Elder Elves," Waverly supplied. "I heard they did it last year. I also head some of the ladies almost got into a fight over the affection of your friend."

It wouldn't surprise Dominic one bit. "Do you sing here often?"

Waverly pointed toward the crown. "Part of the job duties, not like I'm complaining or anything. I get to sing and hang out with these wonderful folks."

"Ho, ho, ho," a chubby Santa bellowed on his way over to them. "Hello, pretty lady."

Dominic didn't know who Ascot thought he was fooling. He steeled himself in place, shoving his hands into the front of his khaki slacks. Waverly stood closer to Dominic.

"Anson." Waverly acknowledged the mayor with a icy smile. The temperature dropped with her tone.

"Ah, ah, ah." Anson wagged his white-gloved hands in her direction. "I'm Santa. You best remember or you'll go on my naughty list. Or perhaps…"

"Wait a damn minute, now," Dominic growled, stepping forward. He extracted his hands and pressed one against Anson's chest. Waverly pressed hers on Dominic's biceps.

"Gentlemen," she said under her breath, "let's remember where we are and why we're here."

"I'm here to do a job," said Anson. "Waverly, I know why you're here, blessing us with your heavenly voice and angelic presence. *Mr. Waverly*, why are you here? Carrying her bags or here to polish her crown?"

Dominic ground his back teeth and wondered what kind of scandal he would cause for Waverly and the committee if he punched Ascot in the throat right now.

"Dominic," Mr. Myers called out over the heads of three ladies. "Come over here and meet some of my friends. Bring yours."

There was no way in hell Dominic was going to hang out with Anson this afternoon. "Maybe some other time," he said. "I better get back to the garage."

"What a shame," Anson said.

Dominic turned before he said something or did something to reiterate what Anson thought of him. He headed back outside and as his hand rested on the iron railing, Waverly caught up with him.

"Where are you going? We're just about to get started with the Metamucil cookies and prune juice." Waverly's eyes widened and she rubbed her belly.

"Don't ask me to go back inside, with Anson fawning all over you, when you won't allow me to punch him for making lewd comments."

"What does it matter what he says?" Waverly asked. "He's harmless and I'm not interested in him."

"Well, who are you interested in?" Dominic demanded.

Waverly took a step toward him in her red spike heels. Her lips parted, then pressed together. She gulped and twisted a lock of dark hair around her slender index finger. "I'm interested in you."

"I can't do this back-and-forth thing, Waverly," Dominic said.

"So don't."

The words struck a chord in Dominic's heart. They were the same words she said the night before last, just before he devoured her body. Like then, Dominic closed the gap between them by snaking his arm around her waist. He drew her close and hard against his body. Without thinking or caring who was around, Dominic dipped his head and brought his lips crashing down on hers. Waverly wrapped her arms around his shoulders and made a small mew. She smelled like cookies and tasted like frosting. Their mouths were perfectly matched. Their tongues worked in unison. The air around them cooled while their bodies heated up. A car honked and someone jeered. Dominic broke the kiss first.

"So, what do we do about this?" Waverly asked. She reached out and wiped his bottom lip.

"What does the Morality Committee say?" Dominic took a step backward. He held her hands and swung them from side to side. "Because I can't promise I'm not going to touch you."

He liked the way her cheeks turned red. "I—I don't know. I am allowed to have a life, within reason. I don't want to give up my dreams of being Miss Georgia and Miss USA."

Dominic stepped closer, remembering their conversation over pizza. "I'm not proposing to you."

"Good."

"Yet," he followed up. He'd be lying if he said he didn't enjoy watching Waverly squirm. "Let's start with something innocent. Would you like to attend this big dance I'm hearing about with me?"

Waverly bit the corner of her lip. Disappointment began to gather in his bones. "I'm not sure. The committee is going to gather the other pageant queens together to get ready for the runoff in Savannah."

"I can take you," he offered. "Maybe we go out on

the riverboat for the Dolphin Magic Tour, you know, where everyone can see us behaving well."

"There goes that Kris Kringle spirit."

"I'll show you what else the Kris Kringle spirit can do if you agree."

Waverly started twisting her hair again. "You're telling me I have to wait almost twenty-two days before our first date?"

"We can go out tonight if you want," said Dominic, "but Alisha told me women don't like being asked the same day."

"You should know by now," Waverly said with a wink, "I'm not like most women. I'm done at three. What time can you come over?"

Chapter 10

There was something to be said about the sweet scent of cookies in the air in the cafeteria at Southwood Elementary. Two weeks after making their relationship public, Waverly had found herself still performing her Miss Southwood duties. Today was no different than when it had been when she was single. The red-and-gray lunchroom tables were arranged in long rows. Each grade was given a table. Each table had a handful of representatives decorating the premade cookies by parents. Random-sized trophies stood on top of a table decorated with Christmas trees and colorfully wrapped presents in the center of the stage at the front of the cafeteria. Waverly manned a makeshift judging table near the exit sign. Children stopped by to say hello and touch her crown.

Of all the times to have to watch my figure, Waverly thought. With the runoff pageant around the corner, she didn't need another roll to pop up. Sure, social media was on her side and everyone agreed they liked the plumper version of Waverly. But Jillian's skeptical voice played in Waverly's ear. *A moment on the lips...* So Waverly knew better than to take a bite of the frosted sugar cookie she'd just decorated with white icing. The scarf wrapped around her snowman's neck was decorated in blue, and now so were her fingers.

Maybe a taste wouldn't hurt. So she took one and it was totally worth it. Waverly's mouth watered for more.

"You honestly shouldn't do that in public."

Waverly turned to her left and found Dominic standing next to her. Speaking of mouthwatering. How did the man manage to make a pair of chinos and a white oxford look so damn sexy? The sleeves were rolled up, revealing his tattoos. He wore a red tie with Mrs. Claus feeding Santa cookies. Waverly licked her lips where the sweet frosting met her tongue. Dominic's mouth twisted in a devilish smile. She recalled Anson trying to make the same joke last week and how she felt at it... Harassed. But with Dominic commenting, Waverly felt a pang of desire in her belly. Maybe she needed a glass of water or something—anything to keep her away from Dominic. Children were watching and the last thing she needed was to get caught ogling him.

"Here." Dominic offered her a bottle of water. The frost on the plastic looked promising to cool her off. As Waverly grabbed it, Dominic reached for her other hand and pulled her finger to his mouth. It was on the tip of her tongue to stop him, but the warmth and the suction... Waverly gasped for air. It was a quick gesture. She was sure no one saw, it but left a feeling she'd never forget.

"You're incorrigible," said Waverly, finally finding her breath. "You know what I'm up against."

"The Morality Committee," Dominic said. He draped his arm around her shoulders, and with his other hand he scanned the crowd with a pointed finger. "I don't see any of them in sight."

She would have paid attention to all the children with their hands covered in red, white and green icing but Dominic's distracting palm made its way down to her backside.

"You look flushed," he pointed out and pushed the bottle of water in her direction. "You ought to take a drink."

"And you need to stop touching me in such ways." Waverly sidestepped Dominic's touch. "There are children here."

Dominic chuckled. "I'm going to need you to clutch your pearls and repeat that."

Waverly rolled her eyes at his teasing. She had a set of pearls to model for him while wearing nothing else. She couldn't wait to show him later in her condo—their secret rendezvous. Her place had become their meeting point since making their relationship official two weeks ago but still quiet and away from prying eyes. With Alisha living in the building, no one questioned Dominic's car staying overnight. A chill ran down her spine with the thought. "Just you wait."

"I can't," he said and picked up the sheet of paper with the list of all the cookies. "You're not going to be able to taste-test all of these."

Patting her belly, Waverly shook her head. "Thank God, no, I'm judging the decorations," she belted out. "I'm signed on for the gingerbread homes."

"I saw the fifth-grade class has a pretty cool condominium going up right about now."

Waverly peered over Dominic's shoulder. In the process, Dominic tugged the hem of her red sweater. The backs of his fingers brushed against her flesh. "You're just being biased. Philly Reyes is in that group."

"Is she?" Dominic made no effort to look over his shoulder.

The two of them were interrupted by the universal symbol of someone announcing their presence: a throat clearing. In this case it was Anson. His black eyes narrowed down where Dominic's hand rested—at the button of her skintight jeans. Waverly attempted to step backward but Dominic held a grip on her waistband.

"Is this really happening?"

"Anson," Waverly began. She hated the look of betrayal on Anson's face but she'd never lied to him.

Anson held his hand in the air to stop her from saying another word. "It's cool." He even gave Dominic a nod. "You told me you didn't have time, so I moved on, as well." He stepped aside and made room for his guest. Vera.

Waverly's upper lip curled at the sight of her nemesis. The official runoff had all the contestants working different events around South Georgia. Waverly was grateful she didn't have to see Vera's face often, but she was intrigued to see her here today. This cookie contest was strictly a Southwood event. Vera linked her fingers through Anson's and gave Waverly an answer. Whether or not they were an official couple, Waverly wasn't sure—but she didn't care.

"Your little cookie event is so cute," Vera cooed. "It

must be so easy to handle in one spot." She linked her arm now around Anson's elbow. A pained expression crossed the mayor's face. "We did something like this in Atlanta, but of course, with Atlanta being so much bigger, it was hard to keep up."

Red spots flamed on Anson's cheeks. "Southwood is just fine, Vera."

"Of course it is," Vera said, not even looking at her date. "Isn't this a shocker?" she asked, wagging her finger between Waverly and Dominic.

Dominic draped his arm over Waverly's shoulder. "Don't start with the accusations, lady."

"I don't believe I like your tone," Anson said, foolishly stepping forward. The mayor tried to stand toe to toe with Dominic but his intentional intimidation was lacking. Dominic overshadowed the man and showed him by dropping his arm from Waverly's shoulder and squaring up.

"Good to know," Dominic said, staring Anson down.

"Oh, good grief." Waverly sighed. "We are on school grounds with dozens of children here. Are the two of you honestly going to get into a pissing match right now?"

"Now, later, whenever," said Dominic. "This man needs to learn some manners."

Anson scoffed, turned his head toward Vera and laughed. "The man with grease under his nails is going to teach me manners?"

The next thing Waverly recalled happening was Dominic's hand snaking out quickly to the collar and ascot around Anson's throat. Anson tried to cry out, but with Dominic's hand around his neck there wasn't any chance.

Waverly gasped. "Dominic." She tried gripping Dominic's arm, but he was too strong and in the zone. Waverly panicked, not wanting the children to see. At least she was able to push the men out the exit door. The door slammed behind them,

Thankfully two gentlemen passing by helped in breaking up the altercation. At least, she thought they were gentlemen. The newcomers grabbed Anson by the arms and threw him up against the brick wall and roughed him up. It was on the tip of Waverly's tongue to scream but she didn't want to alert the children. Vera came outside and started swatting the two men with her clutch.

"Hey, hold up," said one of them.

"Dario? Darren?" Dominic said, rubbing his fists together.

"Alisha told us where to find you," one of them said.

Clearly the three of them knew each other. Everyone forgot about Anson, which was a good thing for the mayor, who slinked away with Vera in tow. "Waverly, I want you to meet my little brothers, Dario and Darren Crowne."

The first named nodded his head and took one long slide step in front of Waverly to reach for her hand. Like Dominic, Dario was big and broad but with fewer tattoos. Darren, who stepped forward next to shake Waverly's hand, favored Dominic the most with light eyes. The members of the Crowne family all bore a resemblance to one another.

Both men flirted with her, taking too long with their kisses to the back of her hands...something Dominic didn't appreciate. "Back off," Dominic growled and snaked his arm around Waverly's waist.

Torn between the laughter at the way the brothers got under Dominic's skin and anger at the Neanderthal act Dominic just put on with Anson, Waverly pulled his hand from her side. "You're in trouble with me."

"What?" Dominic asked. He gaped at her. "You're not honestly bothered by my putting Ascot in his place."

"Anson." Waverly folded her arms across her chest.

"Who is Anson or Ascot?" asked Darren. "The dude?"

"The dude is the mayor," Waverly explained.

Dario threw his hands in the air in surrender. "Whoa, are you trying to get us kicked out of the town before we have a chance to paint it red?"

"He's a thorn in my side, always hitting on my lady." Dominic made one more attempt to reach for Waverly. This time she softened her stance and allowed him to tug her close. "That's my girl. I'm sorry if I caused a scene."

"I think I pushed you guys out before the children noticed."

Dominic hit his forehead with the palm of his hand. "Damn it. I can't believe I lost control like that. I'm sorry, Waverly."

Dario hit Darren in the arm with the back of his hand. "Did our big brother just apologize?"

"I do believe he did," Darren said with a sudden Southern twang in his voice. "Perhaps he's gone soft since Dad died."

For the first time since she and Dominic met, Waverly heard something about Dominic's father. She'd assumed he left or died when he was younger and he didn't want to talk about it. Either way, Waverly wasn't prepared for what Dario added. "You've changed, old man." Dario punched Dominic hard in the arm and Waverly felt the vibration.

"Wait, what?" Waverly did a double take.

Dominic's jawline twitched. "Waverly, I…"

"Your father died?" She stepped in front of Dominic and placed her hands on her hips.

"Sure," Darren graciously provided, "the old man hung on for three months, but he finally kicked the bucket. Gave us a thankful Thanksgiving."

At a loss for words, Waverly stood in front of Dominic, shaking her head.

"Babe, let me explain."

Her heart ached and her eyes prickled with tears. "You've been holding that in all this time? Why didn't you say anything?" Instead of the anger she felt a moment ago, Waverly felt sorry for Dominic. He'd been so strong, her rock. He probably was the same for Alisha and their brothers. No one ever stopped to ask him how he was doing. Waverly stood on tiptoe and wrapped her arms around Dominic's shoulders. He leaned over and nuzzled her neck. "I'm so sorry," Waverly said before pressing a kiss to the side of Dominic's face. She didn't let go of him until a feminine voice echoed down the breezeway.

"Well, what on earth have I walked in on?"

Waverly stepped aside and groaned inwardly. "Ma, what are you doing here?"

Jillian Leverve, in her fifties, didn't look a day older than forty. She never had a strand of her brown hair out of place. Today her mother stood at the end of the corridor, pulling her red leather gloves off her hands one finger at a time. By the time she reached Waverly and Dominic, Waverly was sure her mother would smack Dominic with her glove and challenge him to a duel. Instead, Jillian's eyes cut down Dominic's attire and assessed him immediately.

"Jesus, Waverly, another bad boy?"

Dominic pressed his hand to the small of Waverly's back and a kiss against her ear. "One of these days you're going to tell me about all these bad boys," he whispered and then turned on the charm toward her mother. "Mrs. Leverve, pleasure to meet you. Dominic Crowne."

Jillian stared at Dominic's outstretched hand. Waverly willed her mother to take it. Finally Jillian accepted the welcoming gesture. "You're not at all what I expected after reading the article in *Forbes*, Mr. Crowne. It's a pleasure to make your acquaintance. My husband is a fan."

Waverly wanted to breathe a sigh of relief but couldn't. This meant her father would approve, since he rarely was in favor of Waverly's involvement in the pageant world. So her father approved and that was okay, Waverly guessed. What was worse, her mother hating your boyfriend or actually admiring him? Where was the mother she knew who hated every boyfriend of hers if he came from the wrong side of the tracks? Where was her mother who didn't think anyone, no matter their financial status, was good enough for her daughter?

"It's always nice to meet a fan," said Dominic.

Jillian pulled her hand away and wiped her palm on her hips. "Well, I said my husband is a fan, not me."

Ah, Waverly sighed, there was her mother.

* * *

By the following weekend Waverly had finally talked her mother into staying at the Magnolia Palace. Despite being separated from her for the last six months, Waverly still needed the extra distance. According to Jillian, the condo was not fit for a queen. There were not enough personal decorations on the walls, no shrine dedicated to Waverly's pageant journey on the wall. What made things worse was that, with her mother staying at her apartment, Dominic couldn't come over as usual.

"She's driving me nuts," Waverly complained. She turned the ringer off on her cell phone, then nestled into the crook of Dominic's waiting arms. "I get that this condo isn't 'mine,'" she said, using air quotes, "but she doesn't have to trash everything."

"She cares," Dominic assured her.

Thankfully Dominic understood, or at least he didn't say anything about the digs Jillian had made toward him during the week. After the cookie contest, Dominic took his brothers, Waverly and her mother out to eat at Valencia's, the restaurant around the corner from Grits and Glam Studios. Jillian acted aloof to the 1969 Rolls-Royce Phantom VI. So what if it was the car of many royal families? Jillian found something wrong. She didn't like Valencia because it was too crowded, despite it recently surpassing Duvernay's in popularity. And even with Dominic dressed in two-thousand-dollar suits, Jillian questioned his tattoos.

"She just cares about me having what she considers the best of everything," Waverly argued, then lifted her head on the pillow. Dominic's after-five shadow bristled against her forehead.

"I have the best right here." Dominic secured his arm under her neck and tilted her toward him for a kiss.

Waverly's heart swelled. She lifted her head. "You're too sweet. I love you, you know that, right?"

Dominic shifted and faced her. The words just flew out of her mouth without her thinking. But she did love him. Now she had to wait for him to tell her, "No, thanks." In the span of seconds, Waverly's mind wandered. Did she speak too soon? A lump lodged in her throat. Her insides screamed and fingers shook. Blood pounded between her ears. For a moment tears welled in her eyes with nervous anticipation. She wanted to kick herself.

"I love you, too, Waverly," Dominic answered after ten seconds of torture. Her body weakened with relief. "I don't like the fact I gotta wait so long to do some inappropriate things to you in public…"

Waverly pinched his arm.

"Ouch." Dominic laughed. "Why did I get pinched for just trying to tell you I'm glad you came to your senses and realized how you felt about me?"

"Gee," Waverly gushed with a huff, "how did I get so lucky?"

"According to Stan Harvey, I'm the lucky one."

"The Harveys were here?" She sat up further, pulling herself up on her elbow. "I missed them?"

Dominic turned to face her. Her heart melted. The lamp on the dresser on his side of the bed was still lit, haloing his body. "They stopped by for the Pearl Harbor convocation at Southwood High."

"I can't believe I missed them." Her heart ached. Had they not gone out to the Harveys' last week, Waverly might not have acknowledged her feelings for Dominic. "Damn it."

"Hey now," Dominic said, tipping her chin with his index finger, "such language for a beauty queen. What would the Morality Committee say?"

Heart fluttering, Waverly nipped his finger. "I don't see them around here anywhere."

"So they can't see me do this?" Dominic dipped his fingers below the peach-colored sheet and pulled a nipple into his mouth. The warmth of his tongue set her on fire.

Waverly kicked the covers off them and in a swift move straddled Dominic's waist. He looked up at her with half-closed eyes. His hands rested on her hips. Waverly positioned herself just right, just enough to tease him with the apex of her thighs. Dominic's large hands covered her breasts. He rolled her nipples between his fingers and moisture pooled between her legs. Waverly balanced herself by holding on to his beautifully sculpted abdomen. She enjoyed watching his ripped chest, covered in tattoos, shiver.

"Woman." Dominic groaned. "You're killing me here."

"I'm trying to savor this moment," said Waverly. She leaned forward and slid herself onto his hard erection. Dominic lifted his head and captured her lips. Waverly deepened her kiss. Her breasts brushed against his chest. "I could stay like this all night long." She caressed his whiskered cheek and traced his top lip with her tongue before pulling his bottom lip into her mouth.

Dominic's body tensed and he allowed her to kiss him like that for a moment. Finally, as if he couldn't take it, he grabbed her behind and flipped her onto the bed.

"We'll try to stay like that later. Not right now." Dominic wrapped her legs around his waist and drove in. "Right now I need this."

"Tell me more about your beauty queen," said Dario, helping himself to a beer at Dominic's ranch. "She's hot. Her mom's a piece of work, though."

Later that evening, the Crowne family was rummaging through Dominic's storage to retrieve all the Christmas supplies they needed for the Douglas fir they were going to decorate this evening. Waverly said she was coming, which only made Dominic anticipate the evening even further. He would have his family and Waverly in the same room. He wondered if Jillian would arrive with her.

"Don't get any ideas," Dominic said flatly. He followed his brother into the kitchen and grabbed the last beer left in the fridge without taking out the cardboard container. The twins were seven years younger than him and, to this day, it was hard to see them legally drinking. Even harder to see drink was Alisha, who waltzed into the kitchen and stopped the refrigerator door from closing. She grunted at the sight of the empty six-pack container and reached for Dominic's.

"Youngest buys the beer," said Dominic.

"Whatever," Alisha said with an eye roll.

"We've been here a week and worked nonstop on fifteen cars for your parade." Dario set his beer on the counter and leaned against the stove. "So, seriously, what's going on with you?"

"I'm good, man," Dominic said, avoiding the root of Dario's questioning. "Business is great. Alisha's coming around to being a responsible adult."

"He's referring to you and Waverly," Alisha informed Dominic.

Dominic stood against the island bar. "Thanks," he replied with a sarcastic smirk.

"Waverly isn't your typical girl," Dario noted.

"What is his typical girl?" Darren asked, coming into the room. He leaned forward and rested his elbows on the counter. "I always assumed he was going to marry a car."

"What?" Dominic twisted off the cap of his beer and took a sip. "I've dated plenty of women in my lifetime."

The three siblings shared a questioning look and then started laughing.

Dominic shook his head. "Just because the women I dated didn't land me in jail," he said, looking at Dario and then at Darren, "or get me hauled into the disciplinary action committee at school, doesn't mean I didn't date."

His brothers had the decency to look ashamed. Dario had a penchant for dating women who loved to cause a scene. The last one his girlfriend caused was at a restaurant Dario stupidly thought would be a safe place to break up with her.

"Hey," Dario said, defending himself. "I was trying to back out of getting her something for Valentine's Day. I didn't want her to read too much into our relationship."

Darren laughed. "Yeah, but you forgot it was her birthday on the day you decided to break up with her."

Dominic shook his head. "Clearly I've failed you two."

"Okay, fine," Dario said, "you 'dated' women in the past." He used air quotes around the word *dated*. "You've never brought a woman home to meet us."

"Technically you guys are in my house."

"Dominic, lead by example," said Alisha. "Tell them how serious this relationship is."

"She's special." Dominic didn't argue. Instead he told his family about the complications with dating someone on the verge of trying to become Miss Georgia. As he spoke he felt stupid…as if he were saving himself. His brothers, who used to look at him with adoration, now looked at him with pity. "I'm fine with the way things are."

"If you say so." Dario drained his beer. "Couldn't be me."

"Don't let him fool y'all into believing he's not doing anything with Waverly," Alisha blurted out. "Every night his car's been parked in my visitor's space, yet today is the first day I've seen him."

"Alisha," Dominic huffed.

Alisha shrugged. "What? They're looking at you with such pity."

"It's not pity," said Darren. "I just don't want to see you falling into the same trap Mom fell into when our father was alive."

When Dominic was twelve, his mother went through a rough patch of depression. He didn't know what it was, but he figured she might have taken it hard when John left. Dominic didn't have too long to wonder what it meant; he was too busy making sure the twins and Alisha were taken care of. "What trap?"

"Oh, come on, you know how she never dated, either," said Darren.

Dominic never thought he would be in the same boat as their mother. He dated women. His siblings just didn't know. But it did make him wonder if he was letting Waverly's dream put their future in the back seat.

Alisha scratched her chin. "You're right. Mom is very attractive." She flipped her hair off her shoulders. "Everyone always says how much we look alike. I know how many men hit on me when I go out—I can only imagine how it is with her." All three Crowne men stopped and stared at their sister. Alisha flicked her hand at them. "But carry on."

A few months ago, Will had tried to warn Dominic about the same thing. Waverly's quest for the title kept her busy. But things were what they were and he understood. "Look, I'm not going to discuss my relationship with you all."

"No one is asking you to," Dario and Darren chimed together.

Dominic's cell phone buzzed in his pocket. He wondered if it was Waverly. The clock on the stove behind Dario said it was after five.

"We just don't want you to fall to the wayside," said Dario. "You're no spring chicken."

Dominic flipped his brother the middle finger while he checked his phone.

Running a pageant-worthy errand with my mom; running late.

Dominic swiped the screen and drained his beer. It irritated him she broke a promise. He second-guessed himself. Who was he to stand in her way? But he made a mental note; this might be strike one for her. Dominic loved Waverly but he wasn't going to be strung along. "All right, guys, are we ready to get this decorating thing done?"

Confused, Alisha shook her head. "I thought we were waiting for Waverly?"

"Pageant duty calls," Dominic said, walking out of the kitchen.

Chapter 11

The moment Waverly entered Crowne's Garage the next day, she knew something was wrong. Alisha greeted her as usual, but upon entering Dominic's office, he scowled. Guilt washed over her for not getting over to his place last night for the tree trimming with his family, but his final text before she stopped hearing from him said that he understood.

"Hey, babe." Dominic wiped his hand over his face to fix his frown. He set his phone down on top of his car desk and came around to wash his hands before greeting her, as he always did. Waverly sidestepped him and stood in front of the bathroom.

"Stop." She wrapped her arms around his broad shoulders. "You don't have to wash up before you touch me."

"I don't want to get grease on you and your white outfit," said Dominic. He dipped his head down and kissed the tip of her nose. "Hang on." He slipped into the bathroom and soaped up.

"It's cream. And what if I wanted you to grease me up?" Waverly teased.

Dominic cast a glance over his shoulder. Waverly bit her bottom lip. Any ounce of worry disappeared the moment Dominic's hands cupped her face and he pressed his lips against hers. "I missed you," Waverly breathed.

"You look thin," said Dominic, pulling his arms around her waist. Waverly loved being in this spot. If possible, she'd stay here forever.

"I haven't been away from you that long."

"If you say so. What have you been up to?"

"I've been with my mother on a marathon push to garner support for the runoff this week." Waverly pressed her hands against the buttons of his dark blue coveralls. "What car have you been working on? I didn't see anything out there."

"The twins helped with the cars for the parade, so they've moved out of here." Dominic nodded and stepped backward. "I just sold the Packard."

A cracking sensation gripped Waverly's heart. Images of Dominic's rain-soaked skin flashed through her mind like a series of lightning strikes. "What?"

They both had the same thought about the old vehicle. As unromantic as it might sound to others, the Packard held sentimental value. Dominic nodded. "I couldn't pass up the offer."

Waverly managed to nod. This was his profession. He rebuilt cars and sold them to the highest bidder. "I understand."

"No, you don't." Dominic chuckled and tipped her chin up. Behind him, his phone buzzed from the top of a stack of papers. He stepped back to grab it and swiped the phone, then cursed. "I'm going to kill whoever is doing this."

Waverly stepped over to the Dominic's desk. "What?"

He held the phone for her to see. Another meme. This one was from the cookie contest at the local elementary school. Someone took a photograph just outside the cafeteria when Dario and Darren grabbed Anson and Dominic's hands were still around the mayor's throat. Waverly's hands were trying to pry between them on one side of the scuffle and Vera stood on the other with her hands over her face. The caption read Beauty Queen Knockout and changed Waverly's jacket to a Pink Ladies jacket and swapped the boys' tops for black T-shirts with *T-Birds* written on the back.

"This is crazy," Waverly said, seething. "Now they're dragging you guys into this?"

"I don't recall anyone being outside," said Dominic. "Not that I'm excusing my actions."

"Everyone was inside." Waverly chewed her bottom lip. Her heart pounded in her ears as Dominic stared at her. She feared his next words. Getting his brothers involved in her drama was inexcusable. They didn't ask to be brought into this. Like beauty pageants, colleges held their students to a code of ethics outside campus. Waverly had seen enough news reports about fraternity brothers behaving badly and getting kicked out of school. She'd placed the twins' educations in jeopardy. "Dominic, I'm so sorry. Your brothers must hate me. Tell Dario and Darren I'll talk to their school board and explain everything. This isn't their fault," she rambled, but Dominic came over and cradled her in his arms.

"Waverly, I'm not worried about their school and neither are they."

"They should be." Waverly sobbed into his chest as he stroked her hair.

"Waverly, you have a stalker."

Blood cold, Waverly stopped crying. Panic set into her system. Images of murder victims flashed through her mind, with cut-out magazine letters pasted in cryptic words next to their lifeless bodies. She blinked in disbelief. Surely she would know if she had a stalker. She had no letters, no cut-off Barbie doll heads. "Oh, please, this is probably one of Vera's tricks"

"Except Vera is in the photos with you for a few of these."

"I'm not going to be scared into giving up my spot. I've come too far," Waverly vowed.

"With everything going on, are you sure you want to do this?"

Waverly glanced up from the makeup chair backstage of the Trustees Theater in Savannah and glanced into the mirror at Zoe Baldwin, now creative design director at Ravens Cosmetics, slipping her blush brush into the front pocket of her smock. Titus did not work out for Ravens and the company had to let him go. Last Waverly heard, he was doing makeup web tutorials. The engagement ring on Zoe's left hand blinded Waverly for a moment and reminded her that one day she hoped to have a rock like that. A streak of jealousy washed over Waverly. She wanted to be engaged. She wanted to marry Dominic one day. And she was sure he wanted to marry her. So she had, what? Two more years, if things went according to plan?

"Everything I've worked for," Waverly began, "all starts here."

Mayor Anson insisted that, since she represented Southwood, he needed to be at the runoff. He stood in the doorway with a dozen roses. "Yes, I understand." Anson nodded, but Waverly didn't believe him. "And I want you to know if you don't win today…"

"Excuse me?" Waverly and Zoe, as well as Jillian from her corner of the dressing room, chorused. Jillian set her magazine down and crossed the dressing room in her gold jumpsuit like she'd walked the stage back in the day.

"Anson?" Jillian cooed. "We all have faith in you as a future congressman. Why would you question Waverly's chances?"

"Sorry." Anson half smiled in apology. The two of them got along so well. For all Anson's attempts to show off Vera as his girlfriend, he certainly fell into Jillian's matchmaking attempts. If her mother had things her way, Anson would eventually be governor and Waverly, a former Miss Georgia, would be his wife. "I just want to be realistic. Waverly knows whatever the outcome, I'm proud to have her representing my city."

The last time Anson gave a pep talk to Waverly about her future as a beauty queen, he'd alluded to her not winning. Did he know something she didn't? The Morality Committee sat on as judges and took in the responses from social media. Waverly had been in the lead with the most votes from the public for the longest time, but Vera received a push when the memes from the cookie contest painted Vera as a referee in another meme. Someone fixed the photograph to have Waverly's hair teased up on top of her head and had her looking like Don King egging on her fighters, the Crownes.

"Thanks, Mayor Ascot," Dominic said, coming up behind the man. Dominic clapped Anson so hard on the shoulder, the mayor's head rattled. "Leave."

"Mr. Crowne," Jillian hissed, snaking her arm through the crook of Anson's elbow. "Do you always have to verbally prove you're from the wrong side of the tracks?"

"Don't forget a thug from the wrong side of the tracks," Dominic quipped. Jillian, at a loss for words, scoffed. "Always a pleasure seeing you." Dominic nodded as her mother reached for Anson's arm to leave the dressing room.

Waverly's pulse raced as she laughed. From the wrong side of tracks or not, the man could definitely wear a suit. To most, it was just plain black. To Waverly, this was the same suit she'd gone with him to have tailored. Behind the privacy of the dressing room curtains at the tailor's, Waverly and Dominic had shared another immoral moment together. Unlike the Packard, he was going to have to keep the suit and put it on at nighttime to seduce her, just as lingerie set the tone for men. Waverly licked her lips as her mother and Anson finally stormed out of the dressing room.

"Waverly," Zoe said, "you're making my job too easy and too fun. Dominic, you're too much."

"Thanks, Zoe," Waverly said, watching Zoe pack up her makeup in the signature Ravens Cosmetics lavender box. "Have you and Will set a date yet?"

"Yeah," Dominic chimed in. "I need to know when to get the rest of our brothers together for one hell of a bachelor party." He rubbed his hands together in mischief.

Waverly crossed her arms and rolled her eyes. "They could never party like the pageant scene, am I right?"

With a shake of her head, Zoe gave Waverly a high five. "All right, let me go find my fiancé, Will."

Dominic pointed his thumb down the hall. "Last I saw, my brother was speaking with some cousins of his down the hall."

"Thanks," said Zoe. She collected her box on the table in front of the mirror. "I'll see you after the talent portion."

"Cool."

Zoe headed toward the door, patting Dominic on the shoulder on her way out. "See you in the audience. Will said you're going to need a crew to keep you down in your seat during the swimsuit portion."

"Swimsuit?" Dominic repeated. He glared in Waverly's direction with raised brows. "This is a runoff, correct?"

"Here." Zoe cleared her throat. "I believe you dropped this."

Waverly cocked her head to see what Zoe handed him. It looked like a cell phone but it was not his. Distracted by the swimsuit issue, Dominic slid it into the pocket of his black slacks. Zoe disappeared out the door.

"Swimsuit, Waverly?"

Waverly nibbled her lips, covered in pink Pageant Pleasures lipstick. "Didn't I mention it?"

"Didn't I mention I don't like to share?"

The anger in his voice was real but not threatening. Waverly had purposely left out the swimsuit portion in her description, not knowing how he would respond. "It's part of the pageant."

Dominic crossed the room. Waverly's heart raced. He clamped his hands on either side of the arms of the chair and brought her face close to his. "You're lucky I'm secure."

His lips hovered over hers, careful not to mess up her lipstick. Waverly shivered at the erotic warmth of his breath. Dominic traced the pale pink sweetheart neckline of her gown. Due to the untraditional runoff, Lexi was able to design a gown for Waverly that fit her curves perfectly.

"Sorry to interrupt."

A deep voice entered the room and caused Dominic to growl before he stood upright and turned around. Waverly leaned forward in her chair. Her eyes narrowed at the man in the doorway. He wore a pair of faded denim jeans, black boots and a white T-shirt, a page straight out of her history. "Johnny Del Vecchio?"

At the mention of the name, Dominic turned his head toward Waverly. She shrugged.

Johnny stepped farther into the room and closer to Waverly. Dominic crossed his arms over his chest. "All right. You got me." Johnny laughed. "I am not sorry for interrupting. Johnny, Johnny Del Vecchio," he said to Dominic.

Dominic didn't budge. Waverly didn't expect him to. With Dominic's suggestion that a stalker created the memes, the police chief interrogated Waverly about everyone she'd come across recently. The story of her being kicked out of the last pageant held in Savannah had been brought up, thanks to her mother.

"You show up now?" Dominic adjusted his arms across his chest.

"Yeah, I did, considering this was the place I saw Waverly," said Johnny.

"Relax, Dominic." Waverly tugged the hem of Dominic's black jacket. "I told you all before, he's okay."

"The stalker thing?" Johnny asked. "It's real?"

"Of course it's real," Dominic barked. "What do you know?"

"Nothing other than my lawyer mentioning it to me," said Johnny. "The cops wanted to talk to me about you. You really have a stalker."

"Yes," said Dominic.

Waverly stood up and shook her head. Dominic didn't budge to let her by. "It appears someone has been watching my moves and posting them to the web. You look…great, Johnny." Waverly said. Dominic moved just enough to give her a questioning glance.

"Actually I don't look anything like a biker in my real job. I'm forced to wear a suit and tie every day." Johnny laughed. "When I learned you'd be here for a pageant, I knew your mom would be around. I just wanted to irk her."

Muscles visibly relaxing, Dominic extended his hand for Johnny to shake. "Dominic Crowne."

"Pleased to meet you, Dominic."

"So, what brings you to Savannah?" Waverly asked. "Surely you're not here just for the pageant," She stepped forward and wrapped her arm around Dominic underneath his jacket.

"Half-right," he said. "I live in Jacksonville, but I thought I'd drive up for this and see how you're doing. And from what I can tell, you're doing just fine." Johnny extended his hand again to Dominic. "Congratulations to you."

"For?" Dominic asked.

"You have a beautiful queen here," Johnny said with a wink at Waverly. "When we dated, she never allowed me backstage in her dressing room. That speaks volumes to me. Take care of her."

"Yeah, thanks." Dominic cleared his throat and almost turned toward Waverly. His light brown eyes twinkled with amusement. "I'll tell you what. I've got to go meet up with my frat brother. You keep Waverly company until it's curtain time. I trust you won't let anything happen to her."

Johnny saluted Dominic, and Waverly shook her head and smiled. Damn, she loved that man.

"And so you left her alone with her ex?" Will Ravens turned in his theater seat and shook his head. "Are you feeling okay?"

"I'm good," Dominic answered truthfully. He was glad his brother flew in with his fiancée. And why wouldn't he? According to the fraternity newsletter, Will had been able to get his family's company back in order, and the person he had to thank was seated with them. Zoe and Will were expected to marry soon. Dominic touched his top pocket just above his heart. He loved Waverly and knew she was the woman for him. Though Waverly had fought her feelings for him in the beginning, she and Dominic had built a strong foundation based on friendship. Dominic smiled to himself. Even without putting a ring on Waverly's finger anytime soon, he'd surpassed his fears of ending up in life like his father. If Johnny Del Whatever wanted to talk to Waverly alone, Dominic was cool with it. Dominic didn't believe Johnny was the stalker. But someone out there was.

Will's presence offered a brief moment of normalcy but nothing about this situation made Dominic comfortable. Waverly didn't take it seriously and wanted to continue as if things were okay. It irritated Dominic to know the tiara meant more to her than her safety.

Dominic's eyes scanned the auditorium. Crowds were filling up the rows. People from all the Southern counties were here to cheer on their beauty queens. He chuckled to himself, thinking they all wasted their time. He'd passed a few of the open doors down the hall backstage and none of the other contestants had anything on Waverly.

Zoe leaned forward and tapped Dominic on the knee. "If it's the same guy who passed me in the hall," Zoe began with a deep breath, "you're a confident man."

"I trust Waverly," Dominic explained and laughed to himself at the questioning look Will shot her.

A cell phone rang somewhere by them. Dominic continued to talk to Will and Zoe about their future plans. Dominic had missed the whole engagement due to his father's illness. The cell phone continued to ring. The whole situation reminded Dominic of the last time one went off when he was watching Waverly—just this time he was getting ready to watch her.

"I believe your phone is ringing," Will said, nodded his head toward Dominic's lap.

"My cell's here." He reached into the pocket of his jacket to double-check his phone.

"I gave you your phone in Waverly's dressing room." Suddenly he remembered the object Zoe had given him. "Well, it's not mine." He leaned to the side and extracted the ringing device. The phone buzzed again and shut off. Dominic swiped the screen and noticed it wasn't password protected. Easier to find the owner, he thought. The screen lit up the space between the now-curious duo of Will and Zoe, who leaned over to see, as well. Confused, Dominic shook his head. The screen saver popped on and it was none other than Waverly. This wasn't her phone.

Dominic thumbed the pictures icon to get an idea of whom the phone belonged to. Something told him to take this to the police, but he needed to see who the owner was. What he found in search of selfies were airbrushed photos and everything necessary for making a meme…every meme of Waverly possible. Angry blood pounded in his ears. A text buzzed through, accompanied by Vera Laing's photo.

Hey, Anson, heard you came down here to see your girl lose to me lol.

Dominic was already out of his seat, pushing his way through the crowds trying to find their seats. Will called after him and tried to follow. He knew his frat brother shouted for him to stop. For Anson's sake, he hoped Will or Zoe went ahead and called the police. Because he was about to kill Anson.

As expected, Dominic found Anson pacing outside Waverly's closed dressing room and stopping at each turn to listen at the door. Jillian fawned over the man, practically petting his shoulders. Another group of pageant ladies and their entourages stepped between Waverly's mother and the mayor. The pink paisley ascot wrapped around Anson's neck was immediately replaced by Dominic's left hand. He slung the man against the wall and punched him in the face. The contact of his fist to Anson's face wasn't satisfying enough. Dominic threw Anson down to the ground.

"Jesus!" Jillian screamed. "Someone help." Her pleas caused a trickle effect of screams and a stampede of stilettos and sequins in the hallway.

Someone came from behind Dominic and grabbed him by the shoulders, but Dominic shrugged out of his jacket and hit Anson a few times. Anson tried to grip Dominic by the forearm to release the pressure on his neck.

"Are you crazy?" Anson asked. "Do you know who I am?"

"Dominic," Waverly screeched.

Only the sound of her voice gave Dominic pause. He saw her petrified face and came to his feet. Somewhere in the background a flash went off. In his peripheral vision Dominic noticed all the cell phones recording the incident. A blonde figure barreled through the crowd; he figured it was Lexi but at the moment Dominic didn't give a damn.

"This is just great, just great," Jillian huffed and sidled up to her daughter. "You see what you get for mixing with this trash?"

"Trash?" Will repeated and stepped over to Dominic, handing him his jacket. "Now, hold on a damn minute."

"Trash," Jillian reiterated. "You can put an expensive suit on, but no matter what you're still, and are always going to be, trash."

"What is going on, Dominic?" Waverly inquired. He hated the look of fear across her face. In an attempt to soothe her, Dominic reached for her with his hands. She recoiled.

"What is going on, Waverly?" Lexi demanded to know, the Morality Committee in tow.

No one spoke, not even Dominic. He needed to see, hear and feel from Waverly that everything was okay. He wanted to talk to her alone. She had never looked at him with such fear and disappointment.

Vera brought up the rear of the group and rushed to Anson's side. She extracted a tissue from her top to wipe away the blood from his bleeding face. "You monster!" Vera cried.

Dominic didn't give a damn what anyone else said, filmed or did, or how they looked at him. The only person he cared about was Waverly...who stood still, frozen, in the doorway.

"This man assaulted the mayor of Southwood, Georgia," Jillian said dramatically, a finger pointed at Dominic's chest. Two uniformed officers began to make their way through the crowd.

"Dominic, is this true?" Lexi asked.

"With good cause," Dominic growled. "Anson is Waverly's stalker."

"What?"

Dominic wasn't sure who said that. It wasn't Waverly. Her lips remained tight. "Waverly, the phone Zoe found and gave me, it wasn't mine. It was Anson's."

"Where is this phone?" Anson asked. The tissue at his nose soaked up his blood. "He's lying, Waverly."

Finally Waverly blinked and began to breathe. Dominic tried to reach her again, but she backed up into Johnny, whether intentionally or not. Johnny held on to Waverly's shoulder.

"You!" Jillian gasped and paled at the sight of Waverly's ex.

"I've missed you, too, Jill," Johnny responded.

"Why are you here? Jesus, Waverly. Must every bad choice you ever made show up today?"

"All right now, Jillian," Lexi said, taking the woman by the shoulders. Lexi pushed Jillian to the side, where Stephen embraced her. "Everyone, please," she said over her shoulder.

"Everyone," Zoe shouted at the top of her voice. The whispers and gossiping ceased. "If you have a dressing room, get to it. If you have a seat, go find it."

Some of the viewers dispersed. The police showed up but took Anson's statement first. Dominic resisted punching Anson again when he tried to play dumb about not knowing why he was assaulted.

"He's her stalker," Dominic said calmly. "Zoe gave me a phone earlier and thought it was mine. I looked through the photo files for any evidence of a selfie and came across all the photos Anson leaked to social media, including the one from the cookie contest, Waverly. He's been the one doing it."

"For what?" Anson sneered.

"Oh, come on, you've been trying to get Waverly's attention for months now. Dying for a chance to get her all to yourself. You've been tearing her down, chipping away at her pride with the memes, all so you can build her up again and she would fall in love with you." Dominic shrugged.

"Dominic," Waverly said. "The memes started before I met you."

"I suppose I posted these memes to corral you to Southwood." Anson grandly gestured, sarcasm oozing from him with a smug smile. "Get out of here with that, Mr. Waverly."

Dominic lunged for Anson again. The crowd of ladies screamed but the police stepped in the way. "I'm good." Dominic shrugged off their hold.

"Dominic," Stephen said, "do you still have the phone?"

Patting his chest and pocket, Dominic couldn't find it. He couldn't remember where he placed it once he discovered the photos. Did he leave it in his seat? Dominic snatched his black jacket and searched the pockets, tearing the material inside out. No phone. He shook his head at the authorities.

"Sir," said one of the officers, "we're going to need to bring you in for a statement."

Dominic understood and knew the routine. "Waverly?"

"I can't believe you did this, Dominic. You knew I was up against the Morality Committee."

Of course he knew. The damn committee came between their relationship at every turn. "Seriously, Waverly?"

Waverly folded her arms beneath her breasts. "You need to leave."

"Waverly." Dominic said her name once more and when she didn't respond, he left.

"I don't know what happened to the phone," said Zoe, retouching Waverly's eyeliner. "He had it when he was sitting with us. Yep, he saw the pictures and took off like a crazed man."

Waverly preferred to go without the makeup. The fat tears threatening to spill were marring Zoe's every attempt to make her pretty. The beauty portion of the show was going to be aired tonight and then narrow down the competition to the top three. Tomorrow, Christmas Eve, those contestants would continue on to vie for their spot to enter Miss Georgia with the blessing of the pageant committee.

For now, the incident took the Morality Committee a couple of hours to sort through. Sponsors pulled out of tomorrow's live event and without them, the pageant would lose funding. Lexi ended up bringing in her sister-in-law, Amelia Reyes, to help call in a few television network favors. While they waited for a ruling, Waverly ended up sending her mother out of the dressing room. The rest of the pageant would be aired tomorrow. Tonight they would film the beauty rundown, where the Southern contestants would each introduce themselves with small, one-minute reels of their lives in the counties they represented and splice it into the live show for tomorrow. Waverly wasn't sure of the professional jargon but she took Amelia's word for it. Knowing it was going to take a few more hours before she found out if she made it to the top three, Waverly decided she couldn't take another minute of Jillian bad-mouthing Dominic. He wasn't crazy. Dominic had a reason to attack Anson. Anson's innocent stance was fishy at best.

"I don't know what happened to the phone, but I did see Vera consoling Anson shortly after everything happened. She could have easily found the phone and hidden it for him."

"What are you saying?" Lexi inquired.

"I believe him," Waverly admitted. A deep shudder pulsed in her shoulders. She believed Dominic. Warning bells blew in her ears. Everything Dominic said made sense. The memes stopped once the threat was away—the threat being Dominic. Anson had worked harder to get close to Waverly at the time. But she'd been too busy working toward the tiara. Waverly scolded herself for not speaking up sooner to defend Dominic. The look of hurt in his eyes would burn her soul forever. She was about to lose the one thing she cared most about: Dominic.

Lexi pushed away from the makeup dresser. "Why do you believe him?"

Zoe took a step backward. "Girl, if you did, why did you let him leave?" Zoe asked, but went on without letting Waverly answer. "Don't get me wrong. Dominic scared the hell out of me when we first met. I actually thought he and Will plotted together to get you to win."

Funny, Waverly half laughed to herself. She'd thought the same thing. "Dominic wouldn't go off on Anson without reason. It was more than the emasculating taunts Anson has been hurling since I was crowned Miss Southwood. But I wouldn't put it past him."

"We searched everywhere for a phone," said Lexi. "We didn't find it."

Waverly shrugged. "I don't care. I don't need to see any evidence. I trust Dominic."

"You do?" Lexi asked.

"With all my heart, Lexi," Waverly replied. "I love him so much that I am sitting here contemplating if this runoff is even worth risking my chance at the Dominic."

"Waverly." Lexi gasped and clutched her heart.

"I'm not sorry." Waverly slid out of her makeup chair.

Lexi flipped her blond hair off her shoulder and inhaled deeply. "That's good to know, because, well—" Lexi stumbled as she pulled an envelope from her back pocket. "When we searched for Anson's phone, I found this."

Waverly took the envelope and looked up at Lexi. "What is this?" She opened the envelope and found a deed to a structure. Not familiar with what one looked like, Waverly sorted through the other pieces of paper. She found a copy of a bill of sale for a 1940 Packard and an application for a Union Soldier Reenactment participant. Waverly's lids became heavy when she read Dominic's name on the application.

"That's a deed for a place upstate," explained Lexi. "Mr. and Mrs. Harvey sold their house at a killer rate. Stephen said the buyer made off with a sweet deal."

"Buyer?" Waverly still did not process what the documents meant. "Why is this in here?"

"Because Dominic bought the house," said Lexi. She flipped the page over and pointed her finger at one line. "He bought the house and put it in your name, Waverly."

"Girl." Zoe spoke up. "I reiterate, what are you still doing here?"

Chapter 12

"I found the channel," Alisha exclaimed from the family room at Dominic's ranch.

The scent of pepperoni pizza filtered through the air. Dominic swore underneath his breath and cursed the fates for not answering his prayers. He didn't want to watch the Southern Runoff Finale, as it was now being called. While other channels broadcast back-to-back Christmas movies, some even the same film, Alisha took the twins' advice and found MET—the Multi-Ethnic Television Network, which aired the special showing of the pageant.

"We interrupt your regularly scheduled program, *Christmas Dinners around the World*, for a special presentation of your local affiliate station."

Dominic stood up from the couch and stretched. "Well, I'm going to hit the hay."

Hamilton jumped from his makeshift bed in the corner of the room and trotted over to Dominic's bare feet. "Alone, pig."

"God—" Alisha groaned "—you're so grumpy."

"Leave our big brother alone," Dario said. "He's upset he was banned from his girlfriend's pageant."

Being banned from her pageant was one thing. Banned from her life was another. When Waverly refused to leave with him after he pointed out Anson's dealings, Dominic was through. Why bother waiting around for someone who didn't believe him?

Blindsided. Dominic thought parental abandonment was bad but at least he'd learned from it. He strived to be an upfront, honorable guy. He'd never thought he'd feel such raw, emotional pain. Waverly ripped his heart out and basically handed it back to him.

"Aw, look," Darren chimed in, "his jaw is clenching. I think he's getting mad all over again."

Everyone lounged around in the same blue sweatpants and gray shirts with Crowne's Garage written in blue. The plan was to get up early and meet downtown for the parade. The fleet of cars left to him by his father was completed and hooked up to floats put together by the high school students and other groups from around town.

"You two are welcome to stay over at Alisha's."

Darren and Dario looked up from their spots on the black leather recliners and in sync put their feet up. "You can't kick us out on Christmas Eve."

Christmas Eve, Dominic thought with further irritation. On top of losing Waverly, he'd lost the Christmas present he'd got her. Yesterday morning the official paperwork was signed and filed. Waverly was about to be the new owner of her dream home for when she retired. Earlier this month the Harveys had come to Southwood and offered him a sweet deal. The only thing it cost Dominic was his time in the future, when he would have to participate in Civil War reenactments with the older guys around town. At the time, it had been worth it. Right now? Dominic frowned and started to leave the family room. His leg hit the empty, open cardboard box.

"You guys clean up this mess," Dominic barked.

"We'll clean it," said Dario, "in the morning. We have some more pizza on the way."

The doorbell rang just as an announcer on the television said, "Live from Savannah!"

"I'll get that." Dario jumped to his feet, almost pushing Dominic out the way. "When they say fast, they mean fast."

In the meantime, Dominic picked up the empty pizza box to make room for the new one. On his way into the kitchen with the garbage, he flipped off the light in the family room, leaving it in the glow of the television and the flickering lights on the Douglas fir tree the family had decorated. When he returned to the living room, he caught a glimpse of Lexi Reyes being interviewed. Dario stood in the archway and cleared his throat.

"Hey, uh, 'lisha and Darren, let's go pick up that pizza."

"What? Why?" Alisha whined. "Wasn't that the pizza guy at the door?"

"No, just me."

Dominic's heart crashed against his rib cage. "Waverly?"

"I would have come sooner, but do you know how hard it is to get an Uber driver on Christmas Eve? Everyone had plans and commitments with the pageant and could not bring me last night. My own mother wouldn't speak to me."

"How did you get here?" Dominic asked.

"Johnny just dropped me off. And if you don't want me here, you'll have to bring me back into town."

"I want you here," he said. He wanted her here more than she'd ever know.

He turned back toward the television, showing the top three candidates now standing next to Lexi. Waverly stood in his living room, in the flesh, wearing a pair of tight-fitting jeans and a white T-shirt with a red plaid, long-sleeved shirt wrapped around her waist. Her hair was down and hung over her shoulder; nestled at the top of her head was her Miss Southwood tiara.

The Crowne siblings and Hamilton scattered out the front door. Dominic crossed the living room and stood in front of Waverly. He wasn't sure how to greet her. Yesterday he would have with a kiss. Tonight he didn't know if should simply shake her hand. He settled for clasping his hands behind his back.

"How is it possible you didn't make it?" he asked.

"I made it," Waverly answered. She held her hands out in front of him, visibly hesitant to touch him, as well. "I had all the points to win."

"But?"

"I won," said Waverly. "I won when I chose you." She finally pressed her hand against his heart.

"You won, but you're here."

"I turned the committee's nomination down, Dominic." Waverly stepped up on tiptoe. Her lips were bare of any makeup. He twitched to kiss her. "I won the runoff."

"You've worked your whole life to be Miss Georgia."

Dominic reached for her hands. He brought her away from the door and into the living room.

"And I know in my heart I can be Miss Georgia, but I'm not interested in that title. Is this the tree I missed out on decorating?" Waverly turned her attention toward the old ornaments the twins had brought up.

"It is. Waverly, talk to me."

Waverly turned her back to him. She fingered an old race car ornament with his name. The gift had been from his father when he first showed interest in cars. "I don't have anything like this in my condo."

"I offered to get you another tree."

"I didn't want another tree."

Dominic placed his hands on her shoulders and coaxed her to turn around. "What do you want, Waverly?"

He didn't expect to greet her tearful eyes. "What happened yesterday will never happen again," Dominic vowed. "You'll never see me reach that level of anger."

"You had every right to be angry," said Waverly. "If you saw my pictures on Anson's phone, then I believe you."

"Why?"

"Because I love you, Dominic." Waverly blinked back a tear. "I love you more than I love pageants. I didn't leave with you because I realized at that moment just how much I love you. I had to sit back and process it again. I had to have them tell me I was practically a shoo-in to win, in spite of the Morality Committee. Remember how the votes were going to help influence the decision of the committee? My votes spiked so high, the pageant closed the polls on social media. I've worked so hard, Dominic, in search of that title. And just when it was in my view, I realized it's not the title I want."

"What title is that?"

"Whatever title you can give me." Waverly shrugged. "I mean hell, what other title can there be? Roommates? Bunk mates?"

At that point Dominic relaxed at her words. "You want to make fun of me at a time like this?"

"What time, Dominic?"

Without a second thought, Dominic bent down on one knee. He reached for her left hand. "I realize at this moment I am unprepared to give you a ring, but the important part of this is moment is… Will you marry me, Waverly?"

Waverly batted her lashes. She pressed a finger against her high cheekbone and pondered his proposal. Dominic yanked her down to his level. Waverly came down slowly, kissing his forehead, cheeks and lips.

"Of course I'll marry you. I love you, Dominic."

Dominic leaned Waverly back and brought her closer. She laughed beneath him and brought him down toward her face for another kiss. He loved this woman. "I promise we'll go ring shopping."

"I don't have to have a ring," Waverly said. "You bought me my freaking dream home. Maybe there will be something in Santa's bag after the parade."

All the parents attending the parade always received a gift in the town square for their children. After the parade Santa would pass out one final present.

"That was more of a Christmas gift," said Waverly. "And speaking of the parade, rumor has it the current person scheduled to play Santa has to bow out due to some emergency dental work."

"I'm not apologizing." Dominic grimaced. "That bastard…"

Dominic's words were drowned out when Waverly kissed him. She tried to roll him onto his back. When she succeeded, Waverly positioned herself right on top of his raging erection. "I wonder who we can get to play Santa."

"Isn't it bad enough I'm going to dress up as a soldier?"

Her pink lips parted. "Oh, crap, I didn't get you anything."

Dominic stroked her hair out of her face. The tiara untangled from her tresses and rolled next to the wrapped presents under the tree. "Trust me, you did already."

Epilogue

One year later

Early-summer sun spilled onto Waverly Crowne's face. She smiled at the memory of her place in life one year ago when she'd felt destitute and lifeless. Now here she sat in the rocking chair on her wraparound porch seated next to Marion Strickland from *Pageant Pride Gazette*, literally full of life. A small tray holding a pitcher of freshly squeezed lemonade and two now-empty glasses stood between them. Their time together had come to an end. Waverly tugged the hem of her pastel yellow shift dress and rose from her seat.

"Things certainly have changed for the better," said Marion, tucking her pink sparkly pencil into the front pocket of her purse.

Waverly had welcomed Marion into her home that

afternoon for a standard interview right before big pageants took place. Marion chose to do her report on Waverly, since she'd followed her pageant career for years. Waverly didn't mind one bit that she been placed in the nostalgia archives. Her tiara days were over with and nothing made her happier. Well, maybe something did; she smiled at the way her heart melted when Dominic strolled up the walkway with Hamilton on a leash. When she and Dominic had married, they'd talked Alisha into giving them custody. She wouldn't have time to properly care for him now that she was in school full-time in Atlanta.

These days, when Dominic wasn't participating in Union Blues reenactments to fulfill the two-year contract he signed with Mr. Harvey, he hung around the house in ballers and T-shirts. The coveralls and expensive suits remained in the closet on hiatus. Right now he was scouting places in town to expand his business. Since moving upstate into the Harveys' home, Dominic turned the daily grind of Crowne's Garage over to his family. The twins moved into the ranch home and Alisha kept her condo. They still traveled to Southwood on a weekly basis so Waverly could work with her students at Grits and Glam Studios as the vocal coach.

"Are you sure we can't talk you into coming to the Miss Georgia Pageant? Everyone is dying to see you."

Of course they are, Waverly thought to herself. Not one meme had been created since Dominic beat the mess out of Anson. Nothing was ever proven about Dominic's accusations, but everyone had their answer. Anson wouldn't press charges against Dominic because if he did, the truth would come to light. Marion stood and gave Waverly a hug.

"You know I can't travel right now," Waverly said.

Stepping backward, Marion hiked her purse onto her shoulder and offered a thoughtful smile. "Any regrets about not going after the crown?"

"Oh, I got the right crown, Marion." Waverly chuckled.

"Make sure you spell *crown* with an *e*," said Dominic from the bottom of the steps. Hamilton oinked in agreement. Dominic jogged up the steps, stood behind Waverly and wrapped his arms around her protruding belly.

"Any chance there's a little beauty queen in there?" Marion asked.

After Christmas, Dominic dragged Waverly down to the courthouse and married her on the spot, just as he'd wanted to the first night he arrived at her place with the misdelivered pizza. Shortly after exchanging vows, they discovered they were expecting. Dominic went out and bought every car decoration for a baby's room that he could find.

"It's a boy," Dominic blurted out.

Waverly elbowed him and shook her head. "He thinks if he keeps saying it, it will be true."

Marion laughed once more and bade them goodbye, leaving the happy husband and wife on the front porch alone. Hamilton, tired from his walk, took a nap in the flower bed against the house.

Dominic took hold of Waverly's hand and turned her around. "You're missing the Miss Georgia Pageant this weekend. Any regrets?"

"No," Waverly said, her heart fluttering as Dominic brought her hands to his lips for a kiss.

"You sure? I know this pageant might bring up some old feelings," said Dominic.

"I am perfectly fine with sitting next to you on the couch, watching the pageant."

"Good." Dominic gave her hand a squeeze. "I'll pay attention. Maybe we can make a friendly wager on who will win?"

Waverly pulled her hand away. "The last time I made a bet with you, I ended up as Miss Southwood. What do you have up your sleeve, Mr. Crowne?"

"Dust off your tiara," Dominic said with a lopsided grin. "There's this thing held before Miss Georgia. Ever heard of the Mrs. Georgia Pageant?"

* * * * *

*If you enjoyed this romantic story,
don't miss these other titles in Carolyn Hector's*
ONCE UPON A TIARA *series:*

*THE MAGIC OF MISTLETOE
THE BACHELOR AND THE BEAUTY QUEEN
HIS SOUTHERN SWEETHEART
THE BEAUTY AND THE CEO*

Available now from Harlequin Kimani Romance!

COMING NEXT MONTH
Available November 21, 2017

#549 SEDUCED BY THE TYCOON AT CHRISTMAS
The Morretti Millionaires • by Pamela Yaye

Italy's most powerful businessman, Romeo Morretti, spends his days brokering multimillion-dollar deals, but an encounter with Zoe Smith sends his life in a new direction. When secrets threaten their passionate bond, Romeo must fight to clear his name before they can share a future under the mistletoe.

#550 A LOVE LIKE THIS
Sapphire Shores • by Kianna Alexander

All action star Devon Granger wants for Christmas is a peaceful escape to his hometown. How is he to rest with Hadley Monroe tending to his every need? And when the media descends on the beachfront community, their dreams of ringing in the New Year together could be out of their grasp…

#551 AN UNEXPECTED HOLIDAY GIFT
The Kingsleys of Texas • by Martha Kennerson

When a scuffle leads to community service, basketball star Keylan "KJ" Kingsley opts to devote his hours to his family's foundation. Soon he plunges into a relationship with charity executive Mia Ramirez. When KJ returns to the court, will his celebrity status risk the family that could be theirs by Christmas?

#552 DESIRE IN A KISS
The Chandler Legacy • by Nicki Night

On impulse, heir to a food empire Christian Chandler creates a fake dating profile and quickly connects with petite powerhouse Serenity Williams. She's smart, down-to-earth and ignites his fantasies from their first encounter. But how can he admit the truth to a woman for whom honesty is everything?

Get 2 Free Books,
Plus 2 Free Gifts—
just for trying the
Reader Service!

KIMANI™ ROMANCE

KROM17R2

LOVE
Harlequin
romance?

Join our Harlequin community to share your thoughts and connect with other romance readers!

Be the first to find out about promotions, news, and exclusive content!

Sign up for the Harlequin e-newsletter and download a free book from any series at
www.TryHarlequin.com

CONNECT WITH US AT:

Harlequin.com/Community

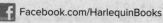 Facebook.com/HarlequinBooks

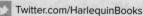 Twitter.com/HarlequinBooks

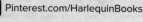 Instagram.com/HarlequinBooks

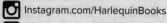 Pinterest.com/HarlequinBooks

ReaderService.com

 **HARLEQUIN**®

**ROMANCE WHEN
YOU NEED IT**

HSOCIAL2017

Want to give in to temptation with steamy tales of irresistible desire?

Check out **Harlequin® Presents®**, **Harlequin® Desire** and **Harlequin® Kimani™ Romance** books!

New books available every month!

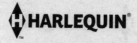

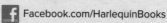
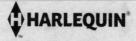

Earn points from all your Harlequin book purchases from wherever you shop.

Turn your points into *FREE BOOKS* of your choice
OR
EXCLUSIVE GIFTS from your favorite authors or series.

Join for FREE today at
www.HarlequinMyRewards.com.

Harlequin My Rewards is a free program (no fees) without any commitments or obligations.

MYR17